I WILL RETURN -TO ME

SHALJAMI AYESHA AHMED

INDIA • SINGAPORE • MALAYSIA

ISBN 979-8-88869-349-0

Dedication

For Abba and Amme

"My Lord, have mercy upon them as they brought me up [when I was] small." (Quran 17:24)

Table of Contents

Prologue

One year later

Darkness spoke to me in a language you and I know not. Yet, as human beings, we learn to communicate way before we are schooled for anything else—in gestures, postures, and instincts. Sometimes, it's not about the language, rather, it's about the un-rhythmic notes; like a distant cousin of emotion, that one uses. The language of loneliness has strange, strong ease in the currents it carries; it attracts, arrests, and engages with the most unexpected empathisers. She spoke to me about you, although I failed to understand why. Why me? Perhaps, she had observed me for a long time, tasted the salty residue of my ache, my helplessness, my longing. I wonder if it tasted familiar to her, or my smell blended with yours, with all the yearning in your room; she understood the void, my grief, and my pain.

Crouched in her lap, I shed every bit of myself. She told me details, that I could never even fathom. I wondered how darkness knew so much about you. You have been confiding in her? Since when, I wanted to ask? My tears felt hot and waxy with sentiments. I simply couldn't stop them from streaking my makeup. You know how I hate that, right? Yet, there I was, listening to her talk, defend, and support you. I didn't understand, seriously.

There came a point, somewhere midway, when I started feeling jealous, annoyed, and perhaps slightly indignant too. What was the need to share so much of yourself with her? Was I not there for you? I wanted to claw at you in anger. Darkness hurts the eyes most when we close them—did you ever realise? Perhaps it is the nakedness that baulks back at it or the vulnerability it feels at being written off by light so simply; that it rebukes, lashes out at large—like a neglected sibling.

I let my hands be my eyes, rummaging through your bed. I looked for your heavy, furry, blanket; my craving, for your smell, was intense. At last, I feel the rough fur graze my soft palms, immediately I grab it, clutch it tightly, and wrap myself into a cocoon of our memories; almost like a hedgehog—some of them are sure spiny right? It helps me build you; backwards you know, your favourite cologne Lagerfeld; its earthy, woody tones, swimming in a potpourri of sandalwood, rose, and tobacco undertones. I close my eyes not too tightly; flashes of your smile appear and fade, and your soft brown wavy hair I try to mess with. It aches to remember how you admonished me for it.

Memories have a strange way of seeping into the epidermis. Even the unpleasant ones sometimes make us yearn for them so fondly. Suddenly I feel myself laughing and crying at the same time. Am I losing my mind, I wonder? It's like a rewind button that I amble through, relishing every bit of your memories; some dilapidated, burnt edges, yellowed and frail to even touch for too long. Frightened, to let go too soon or cling too hard and drown; I oscillate in the periphery of finding you and not losing you completely.

I still remember how you used to smile and always encouraged me to dream. Your thick brows furrowed together, would shadow the radiance in your eyes, and you would say, "Not anybody— everybody can achieve their dreams; conceive it with religiosity, placenta it with discipline, and give birth to it with ferocity like nobody's watching. It might hurt a little or perhaps a lot sometimes. Mace, in the end, it will all be worth it."

I often wondered what struck you about motherhood that you worded your metaphors in its context. You being a boy that is, how you understood the dynamics of it with so much fervour. When I asked you about it, you would just shrug it off, pinning a joke on it, every time.

Now, somehow, after you being gone for so long, I hate admitting that to myself, you know—it hurts, pinches, pricks me deep scathingly. I found the answer, though! Can you believe it? I understand now, how you used to mirror everything mother said. Between finding yourself and worshipping her, you stepped into a whole new terrain. One that defined a fine personality in you, broadening your scope of wisdom, constructing empathy, and filling you with patience and resilience. Making you a person of such strong character, an ideal man, a doting son, a protective and proud dearest brother to me.

Some days are dawn-less, daunting; I feel the weight of your disappearance weigh me down, it feels like a rope tied to me and a large rock—pulling me into the swallowing depths of the ocean. Holding onto hope I feel exhausted even, miserable, yet I don't want to lose, even if it hurts, scars, or bruises me. Other days are pivotal and unstable, I see the look in Dad's eyes; it's as if he has lost the alertness he once was so proud of. He smiles—only to curtain his tears. I too turn away from him, giving him the space to vent out. Mama has not been the same, it's almost like a piece of her was sucked out and she doesn't even want to or perhaps doesn't even know how to fill that void. She seems distracted, lost, and temporarily unavailable for even me, her daughter. We were a happy family, right, Jerry?

I wonder, how much you are suffering? I don't ever trudge into the road of the unseen, I know you are out there somewhere, yearning for return. No one has given up on you or thinks you have crossed over to the other side; it all comes down to the person you have been. The intensity of your genuineness—rubbed off on everyone who crossed your path. I don't understand it some days, other days it hurts me.

Dad mumbles and prays he will perhaps find you; walking on the road, peddling across the street—whistling away merrily. I laugh wryly, far-fetched his dream seems to me. Even if that did happen, you would never recognise him. With that halo of worry, blame, and sadness that he wears, he has aged at least ten years if not more.

Mama's health improves and deteriorates like the four seasons in our town. There are days when she seems radiant, and full of hope, and we sponge in her positive vibes obliviously and it feels like—as if you will walk in through that gate any minute. On slightly grimmer days though, there are dark clouds hovering above her; spirits suppressed, she barely talks, just sits or walks in a state of daze; sometimes she hums ominously on our tiny verandah filled with potted plants hanging around, rocking her chair perpetually, rapidly, eyes fixed on the ground. On those days, we steer away from her, clutching on hope, for the storm to pass without too much destruction.

There has been no demand for ransom, no threatening mails, phone calls, or deadlines. The possibility of an abduction case has been reduced to dust. What could be the reason for your sudden disappearance? Thinking about it has driven everyone to unknown grounds that we never even imagined existed. The three of us have been clinging onto all kinds of ropes that we could get hold of in this jungle, the journey of your search.

Of late I feel an underlying current; Redbarrow Woods, our small town seems mysterious. Wherever I go, I see eyes following me; when I track them, confront them at times, they seem to evade, ignore, or simply brush me off. Nervous laughter is a favourite mask around now; strangely it was not like this before. It's like everyone knows something, yet no one has been able to join the dots; they are waiting with their tongues hanging out, waiting for that one person, a saviour to do the honours perhaps? A year has passed since that night that blurred our daylights, forever. Today, sitting in your room, soaking in whatever is left of you on your bed, I try to escape the events and live them all over again. At times there is an odd nagging feeling—like I am missing, pushing back something very obvious.

Book I

Chapter 1

The Disappearance

A sudden loud crash, a mysteriously ominous shriek, one that had a sound—simply had no end to it—arrested the neighbourhood of Redbarrow Woods. Even though it had stopped, it felt like it had penetrated so deep inside, there was no way out of it. It felt as if it was resonating inside the lungs of everyone who heard it. Mrs. Jane Davis was in her study, writing her letter for the fortieth time, with crumpled sheets of paper lying scattered all around the table. This had been going on for months now. Every morning she would wake up, take a bath, and concoct a hot, strong cup of Espresso with some creamy scrambled eggs and a couple of slices of warm buttered toast. With the cup and plate in her hand, she would walk almost as if in a trance, towards her study, place her food and beverage carefully on the centre of the table, and plonk herself on the chair. Then she would eat her breakfast concentrating on every single bite meticulously until she finally wiped her mouth with a white napkin with three roses printed at the end.

After finishing her breakfast, she would latch herself to her desk, where she would start her letter writing afresh. Her love for stationery was pronounced everywhere, stacks of scented letter pads of all colours, floral prints, single tones stripes, plain ones, a continuously replenished box of paper pins, staples, staplers, highlighters, an ancient collection of pens and pencils—which was practically a library by itself. It was a colourful, neat, snug study, warm and welcoming it felt, except for its bleak owner. Mrs. Davis usually indulged herself with extra servings of letter writing whenever the hours permitted it after her domestic chores were completed. Like tonight, she found herself sneaking in some delicious time way past midnight. Mrs. Davis was trying hard to concentrate on her letter. Her mind was anxiously shaken from its roots, the aftereffects of the commotion having laid their foundation in her too. It made her jump out of her chair and removing her reading glasses, she peeped outside the window, straining her eyes to see what it was all about.

The street outside seemed quiet, yet guilty, as if it was trying to point out the direction where the incident had taken place. Looking at the other houses, she could see a pair or two of eyes peering from every window. She noticed something strange, one particularly suspicious-looking house, the Masons' residence. The lights were all out, and in this pitch-black darkness, there were no eyes at any of their windows. She knew very well that they were inside. Just last evening, Polly had come over to give her the freshly baked apple pie, her signature dish, which Mrs. Davis loved very much. She liked Polly. She was warm, talkative, easy to confide in, and an excellent listener.

Was the commotion all in her house, Mrs. Davis wondered? She had been looking kind of nervous last evening, and when Mrs. Davis asked her about it, she had just brushed it off. There was something secretive about her always, she was not the kind of person who would talk, or confide in anyone easily. She was ready to listen, not to share, though. If the rumours were true, Polly Mason's husband was abusive, to her and the children. Oh! Those two were such darlings, Jerry and Macy. They were a bright, courteous young pair, always helping others. Jerry had just started college, he wanted to become a writer, and tell a tale to the world, he told her, his ears tinged pink. Macy had long auburn wavy tresses, and big round blue eyes—a spitting image of her mother. She loved baking, she was in her tenth grade, and she wanted to become a professional Pastry Chef. A nice neat pastry shop she wanted to open, right around the corner. She had already started applying for Patisserie courses in France and was awaiting their reply.

The police sirens started off; they were getting closer now. Mrs. Davis could see them approaching the Masons' household. She was right, something had happened, but what? Soon enough there was an ambulance following the police cars.

Polly Mason was not herself that day, anyone could figure it out. There was something shifty in her eyes as if she was hiding something. What was it? No one could guess. A stranger to herself, she felt like. There was a tornado bubbling inside, she couldn't keep it down. After giving the apple pie to Mrs. Davis, she returned home. She sat for a bit outside her house, on the verandah, the scarlet sun swarmed by a group of clouds, as if they all had come to murmur secrets or perhaps some dirty confessions. The sky looked saudade almost, with flecks of pink candy floss being eaten by the luminous rays. Dreamily, she dusted her old wooden, almost rickety armchairs with her favourite peacock duster that was once so thick but had now turned withered and scarce even. She couldn't wait to decipher the whole monologue he had given the other day. It sounded as if he was in pain, hesitant to unscrew his miseries, and her heart went out to him. He was still so much of a novice sometimes, she frowned. If only she could give him a good jerk, rattle him out of his timidity! She would feel just so good, blissful.

He had come to the kitchen looking for her, briefly hugged her half-heartedly, and kissed her cheeks. She could sense something amiss. He was nervous, worried, and jittery. It was so unlike him, that it made Polly's heart sink a little. He perched up on the marble kitchen slab and started.

"Mama, it feels like we haven't had a heart-to-heart chat for the longest time. Remember how we used to chat so much more when I was in school? I used to share the tiniest inconsequential things with you, I always felt so good telling you anything and everything. You would smile, cradle my hands in yours, and never belittle anything I said, so patiently you would listen. Then, after I had poured my heart out to you, you would miraculously tell me what to do about it or to simply let it go. Sometimes you would say I needed to wrap my own little brain around it and find a solution. You made me think, gauge, and find solutions to problems. You know that really helped me, I don't know when and why we stopped doing that, you know. It makes me sad, did I shut you off or you got too busy? I don't know, we should do it again, I don't mean to bother you—whenever you have time. It would be nice," Jerry said, giving her one of his boyish grins.

"Oh, honey! Of course, we should do it, whenever you want, I am always here for you, my Cherry Pie. Now, what`s on your mind? Why don't I get us a nice cup of coffee and your favourite double chocolate cookies and we can have a nice little chat? What do you say?" Polly asked eagerly.

"No, not today, perhaps later, some other day. I have some work now. You carry on, Mama, love you." Jerry pecked her cheek and ran.

He was growing up to be a fine young man, she felt so proud of him. He was polite to practically everyone, the old, the young, even the tiny tots. Oh! How her Jerry loved kids, just like her, it was like pieces of herself she had rooted deep into him and he was sprouting so adorably. There was something strange on his mind lately, she couldn't place a finger on it. From the beginning, with Jerry, she could always sense when something was wrong with him. Even as a baby, she knew his hunger cry, his puckered lips drooped when he fell sick, he let out a tormented cry when he couldn't sleep. It was like she could smell his despair, from faraway, even when he was in boarding school and he would speak to her on the phone. She would know when he was in trouble, missing her, or even worried about his studies.

This time she simply couldn't put a finger on it. It had all started a few days back. For some reason, she had been ignoring it all these days, praying it was normal for a new kid making new friends at college. When he came back home that night, after college, his eyes looked sunken and red, there were lacerations on his hands, and he was limping too. Polly was in the kitchen busy with supper; roast chicken in the oven, mashed potatoes, and caramelised carrots with warm bread rolls. When she saw Jerry, an unusual fear engulfed her, cold sweat beads haloed on her forehead, and her hands and feet were numb, almost piercing her. He was in a hurry, his head bent down, zipping past the drawing room. As if he simply didn't want to be seen by anyone. Polly stood by the refrigerator, watching him closely. She didn't run after him, like she actually wanted to. She knew he would simply brush her off, so she let the door bang into her accelerating heartbeat, while she dug her face into the chiller with her eyes closed tight.

"Mama! What's for dinner?" screamed Macy, jumping out of her room, and prancing around the cream-coloured sofa in front of the television. "You know I saw this really amazing recipe about raspberry panna cotta with dots of wasabi in it, I so want to try it! Don't you think it sounds simply delicious, I so love trying these odd combinations, you know right?" yapped Macy.

Suddenly, she realised her mother was far away, she simply hadn't heard a thing she had said. The mashed potatoes were looking overdone and she was still at it. Her mother made the best mashed potatoes ever, it was quite unbelievable that she had not noticed they were overdone. Biting her lower lip, she put her hand over her mother's, to stop her, switching off the gas simultaneously. Polly jerked back from her thoughts.

"Mace! When did you come? I… uh... didn't realise, what time is it? Is it late already? Go call Jerry, dinner is ready, and then come help me lay the table, love," said Polly.

"Mama, are you alright, is something the matter? Don't worry about dinner, you need some rest, sit down, drink some water and I'll take care of dinner. After dinner, we'll sit and chat, alright?" Macy comforted her mother, rubbing her shoulders.

Polly sighed, sat down to drink some water, and just then, her eyes fell on the mashed potatoes. "Oh, my goodness!" She exclaimed.

How was that possible? She had ruined them, her mind was elsewhere, she cringed inwardly. That's why Mace was concerned, she realised.

Suddenly she felt tired and withered. she simply couldn't let herself be like this, she had to find out what was wrong with Jerry. The night seemed long and laborious; it didn't feel like a night for rest. There was something ominous about the absconding moon, the clouds outside looked skinny, starved too, as if they just wanted to get over with the night. Starless, not one single star could she see from her window. Were they suspicious like her, or simply guilty, she wondered?

She was dying to go inside Jerry's room; fingers dug inside her soft palms, teeth clenched, she wanted to hide her tension from Macy. Mace already had too much going on with her at present, with demanding lessons at school, application for her Patisserie school, and helping her at home too.

Just then, the clicking sound of the lock broke her clasp of thoughts, the door opened and banged shut loudly, and feet scrambled around unceremoniously. Dragging his legs, Jack

Mason entered the house. Mumbling gibberish, he managed to avoid both his wife and daughter and stepped into the bedroom, crashing onto the bed. Jack Mason was a broad-shouldered, tall man, with solemn, serious brown eyes, a mouth that found smiling slightly tedious, and easily blushed at compliments.

He was a warm, loving, and caring man. He liked to spend time with his kids, go on holidays with them, play board games, and take them for ice creams and dinner. When he fell in love with Polly she was working in a restaurant. He started wooing her and that was it for him. She was the most gorgeous girl he had ever laid eyes on. With her long auburn wavy tresses, and a warm smile that attracted all the cold lonely souls. Her big round blue eyes would convince you to lay yourself bare in front of her. It was almost twenty years now. During that time, things had cracked a little; but there was nothing that couldn't be fixed though, he believed that too.

Lately, Jack was having problems at his firm, there was a lot of pressure, and a lot of competition too. He had been forced to work overtime, and as a result, he hardly spent time with his family. He had even heard rumours, about him striking Polly. Of course, that was not true. It hurt him so much to hear those spiteful remarks; that somehow flew at him. He never understood what people got from gossiping about others.

"Jack, honey, come for dinner. It's ready, we're all waiting for you," Polly yelled from the dining room. She received no response, and gathered from it, that he must be fast asleep already.

"Mace, did you check on Jerry yet, why hasn't he come for dinner?"

"Mama, he has fallen asleep, he won't budge even, says he's tired," Macy announced, dragging the chair out to sit at the dining table.

That was not good, Polly felt even more worried about him.

"Even Dad has slept already. It's only both of us left to eat. Let's eat and wrap up the kitchen," Polly resigned quietly.

"Since we are alone, can I ask you what has got you so worried, that the mashed potatoes were overdone? You have never done that, as far as I remember, Mama. You know you can talk to me. Is it Dad? Are you worried about him? Or is it something else? What is playing on your mind? Please talk to me," Macy inquired.

"Oh! Don't worry darling, it's nothing, I must be getting old you know. My body aches and I can see greys sprouting around rapidly. You tell me, how was school, did you get any response from the colleges you applied to? I haven't spoken to Jerry since he got back today. Did you get a chance to talk to him today?" Polly prodded.

"No! I haven't spoken to him today. He seemed occupied. Got a couple of letters from the colleges, not yet decided which one to finalise yet. I thought I'll discuss it with all of you and then take a call," Macy replied.

Macy's reply about Jerry further worried Polly. As they cleared up after dinner, she decided to speak with him, first thing in the morning. It was getting late and she was exhausted too. They hugged goodnight and Macy retired to her room. Polly switched off the lights and also retired to her room.

It was then that it all exploded. Polly had barely touched her head to her pillow when that loud crash and ominous shriek thundered across the room. Jack mumbled something in his sleep and suddenly jerked up from his bed. They both ran across the hall, to see what all the noise was about.

* * *

Chapter 2

The Police Search

The night was in full bloom, it had undressed every bit of the day, stripping it of all the brightness, the colours. Now, it had fangs out, ready to gorge on the timid and the innocent. The sky was clear; the dreariness of the darkness had driven away the piousness of the expanse. Clouds seemed to have scurried off in a hurry as if they didn't want to get bullied by the evil clicking its tongue. The stars too seemed weary, dull, and thoughtful. They twinkled as if they were held at gunpoint. Somehow the wind mistook the complete scenario and was softly humming with a calmness that stilled every bit of the rising tension. This was just the beginning. The unrest of the night was whirring, wandering around to enter a household that was quite oblivious to the storm coming their way.

Polly and Jack banged on the doors of Jerry and Macy respectively. Macy put on her dressing gown and jostled with the lock in a hurry to open the door. Rubbing her eyes, she yawned unabashedly, a slight frown playing on her forehead. Staring at her father, she stood with a questioning look, it did seem as though she had not heard a sound even. She was the soundest sleeper in the family. Polly was not having much luck with Jerry. Though her banging continued, there was absolutely no response from Jerry. Perhaps he was asleep, she thought to herself. Although there was something uncomfortable gnawing at her. In the meantime, Jack and Macy also joined her. Jack had already shared with Macy the odd crashing sound and the shriek they had heard.

"What happened, he still hasn't opened the door. Did you try on his cellphone? Perhaps that might wake him up. I'll go get my phone," Jack said before rushing back to his bedroom, wide awake now, with all the distress at hand.

Macy hugged her mother from behind; she felt her shudder under her embrace. This was all too much for Polly to bear. She started weeping loudly, blabbering gibberish, unfinished sentences drowned in an emotional riot. Macy held her tight and tried to calm her down. She knew how worried their mother got, when they fell sick, were in trouble, or even were upset.

"Mama! Please don't worry, Jerry is such a sleepy head, he must be sleeping with music in his ears, for all we know," Macy tried to convince her wryly.

Jack came running back with his phone and said, "He's not answering, I think I need to break open the door, that's the only alternative."

Polly started wailing even more loudly. Macy quietened and looked worried too by now. Had something bad happened to her dearest brother? Glimpses of his face played in front of her, Jerry teasing her at the breakfast table, both of them playing scrabble together, his warm hug she could still feel when they had a big fight and reconciled finally after two days. She loved him so dearly, it was simply unimaginable that something bad could have happened to him.

Running from arm's length, Jack hit his shoulder to the door several times, until finally, he managed to break the door open. In the meantime, sirens went off from all directions. The commotion had probably led someone to call the cops. They seem to have figured out that it was from their house. For a few seconds, the Masons panicked, forgetting to enter Jerry's room even. Macy and Jack ran towards the front door, while Polly in a dazed state entered his room.

She frantically looked for Jerry on the bed. The room welcomed her with a gush of suffocating smoke. A pungent, repulsive odour filled her senses, almost making her puke and faint at the same time. Things were lying on the floor, clothes from the cupboard scattered on the floor, the shards of the broken mirror making a wreath around his bed. The window was open, she noticed, as she carefully made her way to the bed. The bed looked dishevelled, as if there had been some sort of resistance or scuffle on it. Polly was crying uncontrollably by now, the stream of tears turning into a thunderous waterfall. She could barely see anything through them.

Frantically, she pulled off the covers, screaming for Jerry. With the bed completely stripped off, she realised Jerry was nowhere to be found. The shock of this revelation was too much to bear for her. In a maddening fervour of denial, she bit the pillow hard, putting all her strength into it. She didn't let go of it. Exhausted from all the strength she put in and the trauma she denied facing, she was left bereft of blood in her veins. Within seconds she collapsed on the bed.

Jack and Macy met the police at the front porch, a threatening silence weighing down outside, with the sirens having gone off. The police stood hungrily, like watchdogs growling under their breath. They banged the door noisily, impatiently hovering around the front door.

"The neighbours heard some odd noise coming from your place, I believe. Is everything alright? Can we take a look inside, Mr. Mason, if you don't mind, please?" badgered Chief Grant.

"Yes, we too heard the noise, Officer. We were asleep when it happened, just trying to figure out..." explained Jack. He was interrupted by four police officers, as they barged into the house, webbing their house completely.

"We need to call the ambulance asap, a lady is lying unconscious on the bed," exclaimed Officer Scott into his phone, after finding Polly on the bed.

They had all rushed to Jerry's room by now, and Macy broke down seeing her mother lying immobile. Then realisation struck and she screamed, "Mama! What happened? She was fine right now; she was just waiting for Jerry to open the door. Jerry! Where is my brother? He was supposed to be here asleep, he's not here. Look, that window is open, and his room is never this messy. Dad!" Macy ran to hug her father.

Jack comforted her while he himself was in a distraught state, what with Jerry disappearing and Polly lying unconscious on the bed. He spoke solemnly to Chief Grant, who seemed to be in charge, helping him with whatever information he could.

Meanwhile, the ambulance arrived and they took Polly to it on a stretcher. Macy trailed behind and sat beside her mother, who was still unconscious. Mrs. Davis watched the ambulance leave with Macy and the stretcher with a body on it. She suddenly felt very concerned about the family. *What could have happened to them?* she wondered shivering. She couldn't decide if she should go to visit the house or simply call them on phone. After a lot of contemplation, she decided to call on Macy's cell phone. After the third call was rejected, Macy finally picked up the phone.

"Hello, Mrs. Davis, I am sorry I am not in a state to talk right now. Please, can I talk to you later?" whimpered Macy.

"Macy, dear! I saw you entering the ambulance. Is somebody hurt? I don't mean to bother you, just want to be of any help if I can. You don't worry, it's all going to be alright. You know what, I am coming to the hospital, to be with you, right away," Mrs. Davis concluded.

Hearing her kind voice broke every dam of restraint inside Macy and she started sobbing loudly, filling in all the details, “It’s Mama! We found her unconscious on Jerry’s bed while Dad and me had gone to answer the door. And you know what, Mrs. D, we can’t find Jerry anywhere. Where could he have gone? I am so petrified to even think,” Macy shared and continued to weep.

“Don’t worry dear, I am leaving immediately, your mother is going to be fine, okay? The Police will surely find Jerry. He is a good boy, perhaps he will come back on his own. Must have just gone to get some air, you kids these days tend to do random things like that, right?” Mrs. Davis found herself trying to convince Macy.

Meanwhile, at the Masons’ household, the team of police officers searched Jerry’s room for samples, clues that might have been left behind. They did the necessary procedural questioning about the whereabouts of Jerry Mason, details of his friends, school, relatives, and anyone else he had clashed with recently. Jack gave them all the details that might help in finding his son. Inside he was in a state of disillusionment, dispirited, crouching with slumped shoulders. His son’s belongings were all there, nothing was missing; even his cell phone. It was strange, anybody in this day and age would never leave home without their phone. Assuming that he had left on his own, of course.

* * *

For the next two weeks, the police officers searched in and around the neighbourhood. Chief Albert Grant, the Chief in charge, was in his late forties, with a round face, a big inquisitive set of eyes, and a receding hairline creeping into a balding pate. His torso was large in comparison to his legs, and his left leg had an iron rod, having lost it during a shootout in another posting. He was married with two boys, the first one being the same age as Jerry.

At his game he was good, for he had the nose of a fox; that smelled anything devious or foul from the crime scene itself. He was sitting at his desk, trying to deduce the missing link in this whole scenario. Concentrating hard, something was nagging him, something obvious, yet he just couldn't place a finger on it yet. Just then his junior strolled in. Officer Scott banged a pile of files on his desk and sighed heavily.

"This is outrageous! I have been in and around the neighbourhood for the umpteenth time, yet all they have to say are good things about the boy. It just doesn't seem to add up as a case of something illegal that he might have been involved in, Chief," Scott chimed in.

"Did you check with the college authorities, teachers, friends, girlfriends, perhaps? What about the

fingerprints in the room? It's been two weeks already! I want it like yesterday! If you can't find

something, you're looking in the wrong place. Must I reiterate this every time? Go on now, get to

work," Grant huffed.

Seeing his Chief in a bad mood, Scott got up awkwardly, nodded, saluted, and left. *What has got into him now?* he wondered. Normally, he was friendly, open to discussion, and shared his point of view too. He left without another word, promptly getting down to business.

In his office, Grant ran his fingers through his hair, gritting his teeth, stubbed his cigarette, annoyed at his own rude response to Scott, and even more irritated with the case. By now, he had completely lost his trail of thoughts on it. In resignation, grabbing his stuff, he left for home.

The small town of Redbarrow had never been placed on the map of crime. The people of this town lived honestly, working hard, and spending time with family. None had much ambition or aspirations, each one scrambled, crawled through school and university, and got employed one way or the other without much fuss. They redefined the territory, their domain of living with contentment. As a result, crime rates were negligible, and the police were plump and merry too.

This incident had left a sharp scar on the small town, pulsing to death. Many rumours were doing the rounds about Jerry here. Although he was an example all the parents set in front of their children, suddenly no one was quite so sure as to who he really was. *Was his image tainted behind the mask he wore in front of them?* Some said he was involved in drug marketing, others said he was killed by a jealous lover. *If so, where was the body, did someone bury him alive or perhaps burn him in the thick forest behind Redbarrow?* It was said the forest was centuries old, guarded by White Ash Trees, Mahogany Trees, and Oak trees. Legends said there were eyes in those woods, and those pairs of eyes could witness everything even in the abyss of nothing at all. The leaves crunched and whirred as if completely aware of being watched.

Folklores were impregnated with magic in this forest, none could enter alone, for the brave and mighty had tried and never returned whole. The wild beasts ruled here, generations had lived on with no fear, unseen by human eyes. At the end of this forest, there was a river, which the town wore like a necklace, meandering around its contours.

Chapter 3

Grief – An Uninvited Guest

Five months have passed since that day.

Polly Mason was discharged after a couple of days. She suffers from acute anxiety syndrome. She has never been stable since. She has to go for regular visits to the doctor and relies heavily on medication too. Jack Mason, since that day, has been doing the rounds of the Police Station, with no luck in finding his son. His drinking stopped and his overgrown beard and faded clothes make him look ten years older than he actually is. There is something about losing a child, missing or otherwise, that makes the parent break and reassemble into a different person altogether. A stranger he dons, cloaks within himself, a lost parent trying to find the responsible father in himself. Invariably blaming himself for that which he may or may not have been responsible for. He spends his days working hard at the advertising agency, meeting clients, rebooting game plans, meeting deadlines, and doing overtime. Nights are however different. The darkness tilts the hourglass on grief, he spends time taking care of his ailing wife, tries to talk, and to lighten the load on Macy. In vain, though. She hardly responds to him anymore, lost in her own thoughts.

Grief is the most personal emotion a person experiences. Even if a family experiences a loss of a similar kind, their voyage of grieving can be strangely very different. At first, it is volatile anger bubbling inside, the need to vent out feels imperative. Each one falls into a different zone of explosion, applying mechanisms that they see best fit. Some find comfort in measures to destroy themselves by resorting to destructive means, swaying away in the waves of pessimism. A void that they crave to fill by artificial means. While others, constructively build a wall, to never be broken again. Stoic, ruthless they seem to the world at large, yet inside, the dam built threatens to shatter any second. Some wallow; resort to drowning in this sea of melancholy, questioning the unfairness of it, making them spiteful and jealous of those who they think are luckier than themselves.

None can be judged on the routes they decide to take; they are merely circumstantial. Together they coup into these separate chambers. Torn, each one tries to break out from these chambers, yet they fear what lies outside this abyss. So comfortable they are in the darkness, that they are afraid of the light, to face the drill, the closure which they seek, or perhaps run away from. Such was the state in the Masons' household too.

The police have not been able to locate Jerry, having reached a dead end with the clues. Having found no blood stains or hand prints, except for the immediate family members, all others have stamped and closed the file—as an unsolved mystery. The family members, relatives, and school friends are in a state of shock.

Mrs. Davis had always been a good friend of Polly's. That night, after she was admitted to the hospital, she dropped by every day to the hospital as well as brought food for the family. She had been a strength that Macy and Polly both could rely on and had started depending more on her than ever before. The rest of the neighbours would peep and pry, at times drop by with a random excuse to visit Polly, and actually be lapping up any malicious trail they could exaggerate and blow into speculations. Even a misconstrued argument would heat up their otherwise, dry brittle ladies' nights. Mrs. Davis was of course never invited to these sort of exclusive cookouts or get-togethers, not that it bothered her much. However, she often pondered about that evening before Jerry went missing, Polly was distracted and a little preoccupied—she simply wouldn't tell her what was on her mind. Somehow, that seemed like the missing piece of the puzzle; maybe not, yet her gut feeling was strong.

Now, whenever she spoke to Polly, she seemed distracted and hardly spoke anymore to anyone. It saddened her to see Macy with so many responsibilities too. She had school, then she had to take care of her mother too. Jack Mason was trying hard to keep the family together. Everybody could see that. That's the thing about tragedy, life takes a whole new route in a person's life. The priorities are shuffled, and knocking off, tipping a balance that once seemed so important to their lives.

"Good day to you, Mrs. Davis! I just came by to return your dishes. I also brought a pineapple upside-down cake for you. Was trying out a new recipe and wanted you to taste it," Macy said, entering her porch.

"Oh, how lovely, my dear! Why don't you come inside? I'll bring you a nice cup of hot chocolate, you look like you could do with some," Mrs. Davis smiled warmly.

"No, I think I got to go back, mum is alone. I need to prepare dinner before Dad returns home, he will be tired too, and Jerry will be back from his game too," Macy stopped midway and her eyes filled with tears when realisation struck. Before Mrs. Davis could say anything, she put the dishes down on the table and ran back home in a state of despair, holding back the pain, chugging in the wind, unable to digest any of the grime. She barely noticed the car honking behind her.

She entered her home, ran straight into Jerry's room, slammed the door shut, and drowned herself in his blankets.

The room had a pungent, stale smell in it. Tears ran down her cheeks. The room looked foreign now, a pronounced void filling it. The beige-tinged walls had faded over the months, they didn't welcome anyone now, and they were cold. Like they wanted to be left alone, as if they were not done mourning the lost inhabitant yet. There were webs in every corner of the ceiling, spreading across as the months passed by.

She sat at his study table. Books were lying open; it looked as if someone had been going through them. The police were done with their search a long time ago. Macy wondered who was snooping around. *It could be mother*, she thought to herself. She did come into his room, on the days when she was herself. The other day, she had also seen Dad hovering around this room, perhaps it could be him too.

They all visited his room. Whenever grief accelerated with his gnawing memories, it became a sort of respite, at least for a short while. Sometimes, in the middle of the night, she crept into his bed and slept soundly; pillowed in his memories. Just as she was about to get up from his chair, she saw his favourite book, To Kill a Mockingbird, opened on the dog-eared page. There were some words, a warped message or something, it seems to be underlined twice, with two question marks.

"That's strange, he never scribbles on his books, absolutely hates that, and gets annoyed if I ever do it. His books are precious to him," Macy murmured to herself. She took a closer look at the words. "I Will Return—To Me."

What sort of cryptic message was this, that he had scribbled on his favourite book? She needed to get to the bottom of this, maybe, just maybe, this could lead her back to him. Suddenly she had a mission to go on and all her sadness evaporated, it was as if a faint light peeked back at her expectantly from a broken window. She wiped away her tears, walked across to the kitchen, opened the refrigerator door, and uncapped a bottle of water. With all the crying, she got thirsty frequently. Taking three big gulps, she decided to take a peep into her mother's room to check on her.

The lights were out, yet she knew exactly what her mother would be doing, not sleeping for sure. She walked inside quietly and found her mother lying on her back, eyes wide open, unblinking, staring at the ceiling. The air-conditioner drones added music to the melancholy. On most days, her mother's eyes seemed vacant, as if they simply had nothing better to do. Tonight, tears flowed, some onto the pillow, some more trailing down her nose, in turn invading her lips. Macy tiptoed and crouched on her side of the bed. Gently she reached for her hands. Lying limp on her side, Polly seemed unaware of her daughter's presence all this while, yet when her hands came in contact with Macy's, she winced until she realised it was Macy.

"It's you, Mace, what are you doing down on the ground, come on top, sweetheart. What time is it, are you hungry? I must have fallen asleep. Is Dad back yet? Come on, let's go, and I will make you your favourite tuna sandwich, what say?" Polly said warmly, wiping away her tears and getting up from bed. Some days she seemed completely normal, while there were those other days when she was a stranger even to herself as if she had rented her soul into this body, and she didn't even care about it.

"I am not really hungry, Mama. You know what, why don't I make it for you tonight? I haven't pampered you one bit for the longest time," Macy suggested, pulling her back. The reality was that since Jerry went missing, she had been the one cooking and taking care of her mother.

Polly smiled as her little girl seemed to have grown up so fast. It seemed like just yesterday, that she had heard her crying when she had fallen from the swing. Polly had run to lift her up and hugged her tight, and fussed over her tiny scraped knees. And she would smile up at her, sucking her thumb, feeling loved. Time seemed to have turned tables, without them even realising it had. Tonight, Macy's presence made her feel loved. Macy made her sit down comfortably, while she ran errands around the kitchen to make her tuna sandwich. Her thoughts seem to play dodgeball with those words she had found in Jerry's book. She knew if she didn't get to the bottom of that phrase, she would not be able to do anything in peace. Of course, it was plausible for the policc to miss such a clue, it was not possible for them to know that Jerry would never write in his book. Just then, realisation struck her. *What if it was not Jerry, but someone else who had written it?*

She knew his handwriting, so she was certain he had written those words. Why, she simply couldn't fathom. Pinching her forehead, she rolled her eyes. It was a well-known fact that he used to lend his books to all his friends.

"It just seems to get more and more complicated," Macy muttered to herself in the kitchen.

"What's that, honey? Did you say something?" Polly asked from the living room.

"Huh, no, nothing, Mama, I was just thinking aloud," Macy chuckled. Although she was dying to share it with her mother, she knew it would only affect her health to get worried about anything. *Perhaps it is nothing at all, who knows?* she shrugged.

The door opened and Jack Mason entered, looking haggard, with bags under his eyes, yawning without so much as attempting to cover the hollow cave with his hands. Seeing Polly in the living room surprised him, and lifted his spirits a little. It involuntarily drew a smile across his face. Instead of walking into his room, he decided to sit beside his wife, his stomach rumbling as the smell of buttered mushrooms wafted around so pronounced. Up until now, he had been ignoring his hunger, and just like every other night, he would have gone to bed without any food, yet now he suddenly felt ravenously hungry.

"Hey P, how are you feeling? It's good to see you up," Jack warmly pecked his dear wife.

"It does feel good, I am feeling much better, after a long time. How's work Jay, you look tired, are you working too hard? You need to take some time off, get some rest," Polly scrutinised her husband.

Macy smiled. Watching them together like this, talking with so much concern for each other, liquid warmth usually filled her heart, only now there was a void, a hollowness. A shiver and a tear ran down her spine and cheeks simultaneously. She wiped the tear away quickly as she realised Dad was walking towards her. She held back the dam and arched her lips into a smile.

"Mace, sweetie, how are you? What's cooking, something smells so delicious, suddenly I am famished," Jack said.

"Dad, I am good. It's your favourite beetroot, mushroom, and mutton mince pie. Why don't you relax, sit for a while, I'll just set up the table, then we'll all sit together and eat," Macy said.

Jack helped her set up the table and then they all sat together after a long time, to eat their food in silence. A silence with layers in it, slightly heavy, and grim, yet there was a layer of peace trying to overpower the weariness it had been donning for so long. There was an absence that hovered around, ready to burst open, yet tonight all three carried it with care, evading the pin that would burst it open. After dinner, Jack and Polly retired to their room together, and Macy after their departure slipped into Jerry's room.

Perched up on his bed, she drew the curtains, the night feeling hot against her tear-streaked cheeks, the wind whirring in with interrupted pauses. The clouds swam leisurely with wide breaststrokes across the grey sky, the stars galloped in and out like silver dolphins lazily. There was a sweetness in the view that left pronounced stains at the back of the palate, an orphan pair of hopes, as if walking around, wearing stockings red, white, and green striped. It made it easy for her to believe in the goodness that often runs past the dreariness, that touches the victory line in the end.

Her eyes grew heavy and she dozed off on the warm window sill with the window open. The wind brushed her ringlets into delicate waves against her pale skin. The scene looked picturesque, as moonlight poured luxuriously, accentuating her lashes stained with teardrops, lips parted partially, pale pink, partially glossed. Anyone watching her would immediately be drawn towards her involuntarily. Even in her unconscious state, she could feel the weight of someone watching her, yet her body, limp, refused to lend her the strength to wake up and be more vigilant.

The night never laid itself open to anyone, it only stretched and wrapped its arms, crushing everything that came its way, into the merciless abyss.

Chapter 4

Polly's Outing

I am up in the sky. The soft wind tantalises my touch, and flirts with my cheeks, swinging very high. My giggles are infectious; I can feel you smile, while you push my swing higher and higher. We are both ecstatic, the meadows are green, and spring seductively blooms every flower, petal, and leaf. At first, I feel disoriented, like where am I? I panic. Suddenly it dawns on me, we are in our favourite park. Bunches of purple primroses surround us, and yellow-coloured chrysanthemums border the outer ring of the park. On the other side, I smell the sweetness of red roses, blue Bougainvillea bank at the far end of the park. The orange-coloured seesaw draws my attention, it waits for its turn impatiently; like always we first swing and then play on the seesaw. The air is clear and cheerful; I inhale it hungrily into my lungs. It's been so long since we last visited, I am compelled to think. I was about five; so tiny I feel, and you were ten. Lots of other kids are playing too, some on the ship-shaped slide, others on the roundabout. I try to see their faces, but every time I go close, their features blur.

Hearing my name, I get off the swing, and you ask me to follow you. Happily, I sprint as fast as my tiny legs can carry me. You go beyond the park. I try to catch up; yet I am too tired, so I bend my head down, holding my head between my knees. When I look up, I can't find you anywhere. I feel frightened, scream for you, but no response do I get. Desperately, I start running behind trees, my luck sags, almost morosely. Suddenly I see you, then you fade from that spot, appear on another spot, you fade and appear at different spots with arms stretched, and your voice echoes 'I will return—To ME.' I start to fret, cold sweat trickles down my forehead, mixes with my uncontrollable tears, and I scream.

I wake on the edge of your bed; another turn and I would have fallen gloriously off it. Pushing myself back inside, I search for water on your bedside table, not remembering that you never keep it; neither did I get one bottle last night, as preoccupied as I was. Dragging myself off the bed, I feel a hammer on my skull, doing its job meticulously. I step outside, venturing into the kitchen with my eyes nearly closed, to find some water to drink. Dad is already up and ready, I notice, sitting at the table with a cup of coffee and the newspaper. I check the clock by the dinner wagon, it's barely six in the morning. Since there is no breakfast on the table, I decide to make some, knowing very well, Dad would leave without any if possible. He has started doing that ever since, you know, you left.

The morning pours in like lush golden liquid, through our large French windows. I host it with open arms. I have always loved watching the sunlight gloriously claim its space inside our home. It feels like a runny yolk; a sunny side up, sashed into our living room. The tartness of the dreary night mellows; it gets washed away into the shores of an abyss. This is how summer marches into the small town of Redbarrow. With pomp and show, like a grinning carnival, brightening, heating up those damp corners of un-surety. At the very brink of it, ice cream parlours open full-fledged; with attractive seasonal flavours like mangoes, an assortment of berries, plums, and peaches. They make some irresistible combinations with compelling pricing too. It seems like game time for them. Large gatherings cramp up all such joints; children and adults slurping and wringing the heat away. Watching such scenes, I feel a strong tug in my heart.

I remember us, licking dollops of strawberry ice cream for me and blackcurrant with mint for you. Fighting over the last spoon of a banana split now feels special. Serving the scones with clotted cream and jam, I sit beside Dad. He leaves his paper and looks up at me.

"Morning Mace, you're up early. Did you sleep well, everything alright? You seem like you woke up interrupted by something terrible. Did you have a nightmare?" Dad shoots. He always seems to read me so accurately, sometimes it scares me.

"No, I am alright, sort of a dream turning into a nightmare. It's good to start early isn't it, Dad? What about you, what does your day look like? I hope you won't tire yourself out. You need a break you know," I pipe in.

"I am doing just fine; don't you worry about me. With summer setting in majestically, we have to up our strategies, you know. It looks like it is going to be a busy day ahead. No holiday on the radar now. Actually, it's best this way, easier to be busy than to be not these days," he manages to say.

There is so much unsaid nowadays, it almost feels like a looming toothache. We simply don't talk about what we really want to talk about. We jibber about frail innuendoes, more like our minds, connected, are having the real conversation, about what is really hurting us, bothering us. Just that the words refuse to invoke the real issue. Let's rest at that for now, I don't even feel like dipping into the ocean of your search with the people most affected by you, if that makes sense. Dad leaves for work and I take a strong cup of double Espresso to soothe my persistent headache.

I assume Mama must have woken up by now. Although she always had been an early riser, since she has been dependent on those medicines, she gets up slightly later. It's good; I feel she needs the rest. You were always the last one to wake up, do you remember? You would stay awake late; reading novels, sometimes even jumping between two to four books at a time. In the morning you would wake up, yawning, with untidy hair, and a weak stubble I noticed too, recently. With so much excitement, you would talk about a scene that had kept you wide awake, we would all listen engrossed, excited, and anxious to know what happened next. You were always such a great narrator, it's one thing to be a writer, and quite another to be a storyteller, and you were gifted with both.

All four of us love reading. Do you remember, Mama used to make up incredible stories and tell us at meal times since we were so fussy about food, and we would eat and eat till her story would finish? Bedtimes were delicious, we would look forward to it; she would sit in the middle and we would cuddle in closer to her, like puppies, and an indescribable sweetness of her we would smell. That would fill us with a sense of security—of home perhaps. She would read to us like a melodious hummingbird, lulling us to sleep into a world of sugar-coated dreams.

As I enter her room, familiar notes of rose, jasmine, citrus, and vanilla greet me. Her favourite Chanel No.5. It has been ages since I last inhaled this. That's a good sign, my heart tells me, this is one of her good days. I notice her sitting elegantly at her dressing table, brushing her hair with her head upside down, and I hear her humming. Approaching her from behind, I half hug her and she smiles back at me, looking at me through the mirror.

"You look so lovely, Mama! I am always in awe of you. You know that, right? How do you manage to do it every time? It's unfathomable to me, sometimes I wonder if I have been adopted," I pout my lips and confess.

"Huh! No way, honey, don't be silly now, you have so much of both of us, and a portion of you is so totally yourself. I am so proud of you, my baby. Don't ever say such things, alright? Now, aren't you early for school? I am going over to Mrs. Davis's place. It feels like I haven't been out forever. Did you eat something? I am going to make myself some breakfast, care to join me?" Mama offers.

"I woke up early, so already ate with Dad. I made some scones with jam and clotted cream, and made some for you as well. I need to rush now though, if I don't want to be late. You should go visit Mrs. Davis; she would be delighted to have you. She keeps asking about you, she misses you a lot. I'll see you in the evening," I say, hug her, and run. I leave with a good feeling bubbling inside me.

I dash into my room and get ready for school, shower, and put on a long blue shirt and a pair of beige pants. I am in sort of a pensive mood, so I dress in accordance. My go-to pink sneakers add a little bit of colour, I dab my features with some pale blush on, nude gloss, and thicken my lashes. Irrevocably, my thoughts reel back to those words, in the process. I pause for a bit, and finally realise I am super late. Sprinting my way through the living room, I scream goodbye to Mama and ride to school. The roads are busy, and I needle my way through to reach school.

My thoughts are all over the place, with the attention span of a toddler. I don't really manage to do anything constructive throughout the day. Quite an uneventful day, I declare to myself. My friends notice my spaced-out attitude, perhaps they understand more than I give them credit for, or maybe they are tired of my retorts over the last few months. As a result, they do leave me alone, much to my delight. Today, especially I feel grateful for this attitude of theirs. Somehow, I feel like the earth in space, and that phrase revolves around, appearing and fading in phases. Not to forget, that nightmare to enhance it with your very voice.

After so many months, it's strange that I find it, the inconsequential way I did; not looking for anything and I come across this. Everything seems logical; this clue being missed by the cops. It is such a minor thing; none would question it—scribbling on the book. I need to get to the bottom of this. How? Where do I begin, should I contact the cops? Perhaps and perhaps not, the reason being, firstly they might be able to help me with some investigation, they are after all pros at this sort of thing. Secondly, maybe not, simply because they closed the case—in merely three months. I am just so mad about it with them. How can they give up on a missing person, my brother, so soon?

Dusk prowls into the town almost majestically, it fancies a rusty hue, I notice. The deepest orange sky umbrellas over me. Slowly it fades over the horizon, a curtain is drawn over the events of the day. Ledgers of deeds are shuffled, scribbled, and stamped. Petite ladies with pointed noses, delicate square spectacles, wearing green conservative gowns, hair tied up into no-nonsense buns... They seal these ledgers with a loud dusty thud. Amidst these lies a page about that one phrase; discovered by me, paving a way for me to discover you, I pray.

I cross Mrs. Davis's house and notice the stillness around it. I gather that perhaps Mama must have already left for home. The thought of Mama in good health brings a smile to my face, relief shrouds me, a leaking hope I taste right at the tip of my tongue; sweetened caffeine, it makes me cling to it; she will recover soon. Parking my bike, I ring the bell, but there is no response. Humming to myself, I try to look through the windows; thick maroon curtains stare back at me. I ring the bell a couple of more times; still, there is no answer. Out of irritation, I kick the door impulsively, I am surprised by my own behaviour, so unlike me. I rummage through my bag for my phone, and decide to dial Mama first, maybe she is still at Mrs. D's place, I sigh. The ringtone stops and it goes into voicemail.

My leftover good mood burns like charcoal by now, I am exhausted, hungry, and most of all anxious. Then I call on Dad's landline. Once again, no response I receive. If there was a metre to gauge panic, I would have been tested terminally sick for sure. My final resort; sitting down on the porch armchair, I call Mrs. D.

Chapter 5

Mrs. Smith's Note

After Macy left that morning, Polly got ready and nibbled through her scones and jam. Her mind was not at ease. The silence of the house penetrated through her skin. Every crunch, every scrape of the butter knife layered with jam, grilled her in whispers. Her thoughts were in a relay race, passing the baton on from the void of Jerry to what had really happened that night, to the incidents of the day of his disappearance. There were huge black holes in her memory about that night. Every time she tried to think, her head would throb menacingly. Most of the time, the medicines dulled her memory, trying to keep her from anxiety pangs and choking grief. It was only at times like this, when she was all alone, that she felt this strong urge to rewind and understand what was it that had occurred and resulted in her son's disappearance. None of them ever spoke about it, never discussed that day's events. Of course, they were all hurting inside and didn't want to prod deeper into the pain.

When she woke up in the morning, she felt good, after a long time, so she decided to visit her friend. Mrs. Davis was so warm, welcoming and so real too. She loved listening to her, and Mrs. D did love talking to her so much. In a way, it helped her take her mind off her own worries; at least for a time being. She also had been there for her family in these times of grief. Polly wanted to thank her for her kindness when none of the other neighbours really came forward to help. Most of them would just come to bite into a piece of stray crumb of gossip they might get lucky with.

After finishing her breakfast, she decided to leave for Mrs. Davis's house. She was feeling slightly uncomfortable. A thought was nagging her. Whenever she went to her house, she always baked something and took it for her. Of late, she had not been cooking or baking at all, primarily because of her health, and Mace had completely forbidden her from it, so she could take care of her health. She couldn't find the willpower to bake today as well. She really didn't want to go empty-handed.

In the end, she resolved to pick up some pastries, from the quaint bakery just around the corner from her place. It was a nice place called Baked & Iced. As you entered, a warm smell of freshly baked cakes wafted and welcomed you. Closer to the counter, the strong smell of dark chocolate almost made you giddy with desire. There was a broad oblong chilled counter right in the centre. They offered a wide variety of assorted pastries from mille-feuilles, baked cheesecake slices, signature mud cakes, pies, quiche, brownies, and freshly baked breakfast pastries. Right at the end of the L-shaped counter, there was a chiller filled with ice creams and a counter for waffles for breakfast. This little place was always bustling with people; lovers slurping three scoops of ice cream sundaes, friends dunking into warm sizzling brownies with a vanilla scoop, families sharing a humongous meaty pie. There was so much laughter and good spirit, it always felt like a wonderland. Anyone who entered and exited those thick glass doors, left with the confetti of happiness sprinkled all over them, as if not a dime in this world could go wrong now; that's how one felt.

The owners, Smiths, were much like their outlet—warm, welcoming, and jovial in nature. They had owned this place from the beginning, so this had been passed on from generation to generation. Mr. and Mrs. Smith were kind, generous people and they went out of their way to help the neighbours. Mrs. Bianca Smith was a good friend of Mrs. Davis's and was also very fond of Polly and her family. They had two children. The boy was in the same class as Macy, and the girl was a few years younger. It was in this very outlet, that Macy had first netted her ambition of becoming a Pastry Chef.

She was enchanted by the fluffiness and softness the yeast created in the breads and buns, the way chocolate meandered, melting into a *pain au chocolat*, the tartness held cosily inside a lemon tart, the bitterness of chocolate flirting with peanut butter in a dense decadent pastry. It was a parallel dynasty that she wished to live and reign in from a very young age.

When Polly entered, a familiar tantalising warmth embraced her, and almost immediately she felt happy and positive. It was almost lunch hour and people were trickling into the place, settling in with a menu. Somewhere a stomach rumbled loudly. Not very far, another one was craning his neck to look at how long the line was to give his order. Polly drummed her fingers against the cold counter, pondering over what to take for Mrs. Davis. Quite quickly, her eyes fell on a person carrying a freshly baked blackcurrant crumble pie. She knew this was another of Mrs. Davis's favourites, so she zeroed in on it.

The crowd inside was watching her evasively. She could feel the undercurrent of their questioning gazes. She hated how people were so invasive and not an ounce of empathy dripped from them. It was not like she had become an alien; just as her son had disappeared. She felt sweat beads appearing on her forehead, shoulders slumped defeatedly. Sometimes all this got so tiring, she thought to herself. Just then, she reached the cashier; the line had ended, she looked up to give her order and she met the warmth of Mrs. Smith's eyes.

"How are you, my dear? It's good to see you, you look lovely in that peach colour. It brings out your blue eyes. How are Jack and Macy? What would you like to have today?" Mrs. Smith asked.

"Oh hello, Mrs. Smith, I am very well. How have you been? Thank you so much, this is so old, I just grabbed it drowsily. Jack and Macy are well too, both busy with work and school actually. How are Mr. Smith, Jamie, and Serena? Yes, I'll have that blackcurrant crumble pie. If you could have that gift wrapped, that would be lovely. You must come visit us sometime. It has been so long," Polly replied.

"Why of course we should all get together, it's been forever. We should invite Jane too; she gets lonely you know. Mr. Smith and the kids are good. Life just seems to be rolling on like a rolling pin nowadays; with all of us under it. Here you go, your Blackcurrant crumble ready to go!" Mrs. Smith gave her the packet and slipped a note discreetly into her hands.

Polly was surprised by Mrs. Smith's clandestine manner. However, she clung onto the note and slipped it into her pocket out of inquisitiveness. After collecting her pie, she waved goodbye and walked across the street to Mrs. Davis's house. The sun viciously lashed out, and in a matter of a few seconds, Polly felt exhausted and out of breath. The blinding light made her forget her note and she rang the bell. Mrs. Davis was in her late sixties and afflicted by arthritis. Her bones functioned like a machine that had been dried out, bereft of oil, and cried out at even a slow, small movement. Her spirit though, was quite the opposite, it pushed, fought, and healed at a rapid pace, never once surrendering in this ruthless battle. She opened the door a crack, and as it unbolted, she grinned widely almost like a child who has suddenly seen Santa, and two beads of tears formed in her eyes. Mrs. Davis embraced Polly tightly, laughing into her ears. She smelled of slightly overdone toast, sweet lavender mixed with caffeine.

"It's so good to see you, Polly, I have missed having you around. I was so worried about you. How are you feeling now? I am so terribly sorry about our dear little boy, Jerry. I cannot fathom what you must be going through. Deep down in my heart, I hear him waiting to be discovered. I know, I must be sounding insane. Goodness! Please come on in, that ball of fire is just gorging on our souls mercilessly," Mrs. Davis said.

"I am much better today, so glad I decided to drop by and had the strength to do so too. I have been wanting to come for the longest time—my health simply won't allow it you know. I wanted to thank you for being there for all three of us in these terrible times of grief. You know what, your instincts have always been right and you don't sound insane for saying that at all. Oh here, this is for you, I hope you like it." Polly gave her the pie with a smile.

"Why, you really shouldn't have bothered, Polly, you know you are like my daughter. There is absolutely no need for these formalities really. Now, you sit tight and relax. I will be back in a jiffy. I have made some meatloaf and you must stay for lunch. I will not listen to any excuses," Mrs. Davis said and ran into the kitchen with the pie before Polly could even say another word.

Mrs. Davis's house had a tiny porch, very neatly set up with creepers languorously riding up on one wall, two large bamboo armchairs with red and orange sequined cushions, and between them a small bamboo table with an oval glass slab in its centre. Right at the front, four potted plants were hanging. Inside the living room, there was a three-piece sofa lounge, dusky grey in colour, and in the centre a rectangular wooden table with an abstract centrepiece and some magazines on it. The large windows were covered by thick grey curtains. A bookshelf sprawled into the dining room, which had a four-seater square Mahogany dining table.

Flipping through a magazine, Polly's thoughts suddenly queued up into a row, until one fell out of line, pointing its finger at her and sniggering. Immediately, she remembered the note given by Mrs. Smith. *How could she forget*, she couldn't seem to believe herself. She picked up her bag from the centre table and rummaged through the contents of the bag, finally finding the pink-coloured sticky note, peeking back at her doggedly. She pulled it out delicately, in case it tore in her desperation to read it. Just before she spread it open, she leant towards the right, to check if Mrs. Davis was coming from the kitchen. She heard her humming and the clanking of vessels assured her lunch was yet to arrive. Heaving a sigh, she opened the note. Calligraphic words stared back at her, and it took her a second glance to read them clearly. The note said, "Meet me at eight tonight, at the end of the bridge, just at the beginning of the woods. Come alone." That's all it said. It was signed by Mrs. Smith. She read it again twice, just in case she had missed some detail. So deep in thought was she, that she didn't realise that Mrs. D was towering over her head.

"What's that Polly, is everything alright? You are shivering and you look like you just bumped into death. I'll get you some water," Mrs. Davis said, walking across to the dining table.

Flummoxed, Polly jumped up as if caught in a fishing net, quickly stuffed the note inside her pocket, and composed herself.

"No, I am fine Mrs. D, was absorbed in thinking about better times. Don't worry. Wow, the meatloaf smells delicious," Polly piped in.

Lunch progressed at a steady pace, neither talked much, and most of it was non-sequitur. There was an awkwardness in the air—weighing their close acquaintance down. Polly answered most of the questions in monosyllables and she barely attempted to continue the conversation. She seemed jittery and on edge, and merely picked on the food, as she was too preoccupied with that inconclusive note. Mrs. Davis noticed her discomfort and tried her best to make conversation, being the lovely host that she was, although she herself was increasingly suspicious about the strange behaviour of her visitor.

Much to the relief of both of them, lunch finally ended and both relaxed a little. Polly kept a watch on the time; it was already past four and she started feeling more and more anxious. Mrs. D, sensing her uneasiness, didn't keep her for long; neither did she prod her anymore. She insisted on packing some of the meatloaves for her, complaining all the while that she hadn't eaten properly at all. In the end, Polly gave in and accepted her generosity. They finally hugged each other and bid adieu.

Looking at her watch continuously, Polly decided to take a cab to the bridge as she hardly seemed to have any time left. Mrs. Davis watched her from behind the curtain. Ever since that afternoon before Jerry's disappearance, she had felt there was something quite off with Polly. She wondered why Polly took a cab, when she always walked back home.

Chapter 6

Polly's Secret

A marquee of abysmal circumstances threatens to fall over me in this interim. It feels as if someone is unhinging the structure ruthlessly with a hammer and I am standing right under it, with my head tilted up towards the sky. I watch the nails getting loose with every thud of the hammer, yet I cannot run out, my feet planted in the ground, making me immobile. The interval hovers and looms as I am marooned on this island of ignorance, of not knowing. My shoulders sag, and I feel jittery, biting my lower lip, fingers dig inside my palm, making small semi-circular designs on it. A million arrows of questions shower to and fro, inside my head. The shrill ringtone of the phone matches the heartbeats blaring into my ears. Just as I am about to cut the line, Mrs. Davis picks up the phone.

"Hello, Mrs. Davis, this is Macy. I was wondering if Mama is still at your place. She said she would be visiting you. I reached home and she is still not back. I am not able to get through to her number as well," I say.

"Oh yes, Polly was here in the afternoon and left early in the evening. Has she not reached home yet? Oh, I thought it was strange, as she took a cab from right outside my place. Usually, she walks back home. Also, she seemed quite occupied, as if she was in a hurry, had to reach somewhere else, and kept looking at her watch," Mrs. Davis shares her thoughts.

"Did she mention anything to you, where she had to go? Who she had to meet? This is getting stranger and stranger. In the morning she seemed in a good mood and at leisure."

"No, actually she didn't. I did ask her—she closed up completely. I am so sorry, maybe I should have persisted more. Honestly didn't realise she would disappear like this. Should I come by or maybe call the cops? Please let me know, you know I am here for whatever you need."

"That's alright, I think I'll get in touch with Dad. He should be returning home soon. We should probably wait for a little while longer. She may have gone to visit some other friend, perhaps?" I find myself saying, although I barely believe those words myself.

"All right dear, you let me know, anything you need, I am just a phone call away," Mrs. Davis says and I thank her and end the call.

I hear the crickets chirp, gnawing into my ears. Somehow, they seem so much louder than usual. The elements of the night accentuate around me, while I am stranded; the air is hollow asymmetrically, and a rancid taste stretches at the back of my palate. Something damp and slimy lies on the rocking chair outside, perhaps a dead rat or a hedgehog. A thin layer of mist frills delicately on our round teak wood coffee table. Our coffee table looks like an old bent oak tree, standing on its branches in a U-shape. It has five unruly, entangled legs, and on top of it sits a circular glass slab. The yellow light is feeble, flickering squarely above my head. It's not really the absence of the brightness that they feel powerful in; rather they sense my rising unease, like a prey outside its shelter, cowering under its predator's eyes.

I am far from being frightened of darkness, it's the subtle oddities that seem to wring my forbearance. That dangling uncertainty about Mama... I want to go out there to look for her. I can't fathom where to begin. My first thought, you ask? Hospitals? It makes me giggle nervously. Not again, I plead, squeezing my eyes tight. My hunger no longer throws a tantrum; considerate it is, softly I whisper a thank you to it, tapping my non-existent tummy. I am losing my mind, right? I ought to, by now, I retort.

I am half of me; half is elsewhere, nowhere really, nowhere that you can find and jigsaw me back together. I lose track of the sands of time trickling rapidly by, the invisible hourglass swivels viciously on the nail of my patience. My thoughts are wordless, orphan, stagnant in murky water, infested by time. Have you ever felt this, like a fading bruise losing its existence? I know I need to hold on, yet I don't, won't, can't. I will dial Dad just one more time, this would be the twentieth time, my phone blinks red and switches off. There, my body slumps, like a pile of dirty clothes, without a body in it. I pass out on the third step of the porch, my head hits the potted plant; ironically it is an aloe vera plant, the magical plant that heals all, they say. I mumble something vague, nondescript and that is the last thing I remember.

First, I am on top of a cliff; the wind is violently menacing, I run in circles, screaming ferociously, like I am looking for someone; my heart drones erratically as if it's about to stop. My cheeks are coloured, and I can feel the heat of it. Against the unforgiving chill that masks my view, I am cold with barely a thin soaking shirt that clings to me like a lost child. There is a dark shadow coming at me with full force, my body becomes rigid, stubborn, disobedient even. It won't budge. The battle is a tempest; it's not between two—there are three, my mind, my body, and the shadow. I am going to lose—I can feel it as the dark shadow pushes me off the cliff.

Suddenly, like the flicker of channels on television, I am zapped out. Enter, a black and white camera roll that comes alive, un-reels, there are pictures of you and me, at the school canteen, me crying when I fell off the swing at the park; you console me, you enacting a scene from Macbeth—Dad, Mama, and I watch you in admiration. I am happy and fudgy here; as a spectator. All of us together, the reel keeps running, enlarging as I pinch through it.

Someone nudges me; how I hate being interrupted when I am so engrossed. I ignore it, frown, and continue smiling. I smell something familiar, like mothballs with caramelised honey, and my hands find something soft and furry, snuggling more cosily; wriggle my body under the warmth and blank out—everything fades. I am at peace or merely exhausted—can't place a finger on it. Silhouettes I see; off-springs of the dim light, they appear near me, there are two—I think. I try to get up; to put my weight on my elbows; to ensure I am not being attacked or kidnapped; my voice sounds like a ribbit, in my head I say hey who are you? What do you want? Reality—I am simply croaking. Bewildered, tired and hopeless—finally I give up the fight and fall asleep.

Morning launders in through the window; freshly starched, a distinct, fresh breezy smell, something mellow. Like an elusive laser beam—a malnourished ray falls on the exposed half of my arm. It feels good—just right; with the air-conditioner droning behind me—cool air swishes in and out. I want to laze in bed a little while longer; lick into these little pleasures just a little while longer. The film of darkness sitting on my eyelids turns a rusty hue now, I love how light enters harrumphing its way through. The cuckoo coos outside impatiently; as if it is bustling around and has no time.

Time! Wait, what time is it? Where am I? The events of the night before replay in front of me and I jerk up from my romance with leisure. My room stares back at me—with a sardonic grin, how did I get here again? My headache is gone, yet my throat is dry and I am famished like I can eat a gorilla. Mama and Dad! Where are they? Did they get me back? Where was Mama? Questions peel off me like I am losing skin. The only solution to answer them all is to go face the world outside. So, I take a shower and brush my hair back, put on some clothes, take a deep breath, and tear open the door.

There is an eerie silence outside. My room opens into the dining hall. Empty, it looks back at me guiltily. I don't like silence during the day, it just fits wrong. You had laughed when I told you this — remember? Where are they, I wonder? The strangeness seems to only get bolder and bolder, don't you think? I wish you were here; I peep into your room and nothing seems moved, saintly it pouts at me. I think of screaming, but then I decide otherwise, what if there are intruders asleep and I wake them up? Kitchen I enter next, not a soul… I see a dirty mop sticking out, soaked freshly, recently. Should I simply hide in my room, I ponder? Hunger replies with a growl—need to eat, I surrender. First, let me check their room, my hands are clammy and I am tip-toeing, I realise suddenly—like a stranger in my own house!

The door is left open slightly ajar, I peep to take a look—my head spins one eighty degrees. I don't get a clear view inside the room. My body needs fuel and it would certainly collapse if I don't refill it, it's quite adamant now. So, I go forage for fuel inside the kitchen. At first, I quench my thirst—a tumbler of water I gulp down. Invading the fridge, I notice a casserole of meat pie. Whoa! Where did that come from? The casserole looks familiar; it must be Mrs. Davis's. Taking it out, I simply start digging into it. I am so starved; it hardly matters that it is straight out of the refrigerator.

Halfway through my plunder, I hear footsteps coming closer to me. I turn to see Mama walking out of the room, she looks more like herself today. I run into her arms and hug her tight—before the attack always pamper, right? Then, I shoot a series of bullets at her.

"Mama! I was so worried last night; I came back from school and you were not home. Where were you? I called you like a million times and got no response at all. Even Dad didn't answer my call. You guys are so irresponsible, after what has happened…" I bombard, then suddenly I have brought out the elephant in the room.

"I am sorry Mace, my phone just died on me. I had to go someplace, meet a friend urgently. I didn't realise how long I was gone. When I got back, I met your Dad outside on the porch and you had fallen asleep; he was carrying you inside," Mama says.

"I didn't mean to pounce on you, it's just that I was concerned, worried, and anxious. I am glad you went out; did you have a good time? I asked Mrs. D, she said you sort of looked preoccupied and ran off in a hurry. That frightened me even more. I wanted to look for you, just didn't know where to start. So, in the end, I just stayed put," I share. My explanation is sounding lame to my own ears. I don't know what she must be thinking.

"Did she? Oh! I don't know why she would feel like that. Anyways now I am here and so are you. All's well, right?"

This sounds strange, she is hiding something, I can feel it. For starters, when she said it, she didn't meet my eyes—an evasiveness struck me. I let it pass, and don't investigate further into the matter. Just then, Dad walks in and wants an update.

"Why were you sleeping on the potted plant last night, Mace?" Dad asks, ruffling my hair.

I fill him in on the details of the night and we all have breakfast together.

I have made some scrambled eggs on buttered toast, with fresh orange juice, grilled sausages, and tea. The weekend has arrived, so I can laze around or perhaps sniff around a little. Dad leaves for work and Mama says she has been invited by one of her friends, so she too leaves the house.

I decide to stay at home and un-verse that phrase, although I have no clue where to start. Sometimes, versing is so much easier than un-versing, right? Suddenly, I have an idea, if you were in my place what would you do, that's it! I have to think like you, between quotes, above the apostrophe, tucked slyly under the comma, pressed secretly inside the semi-colon. I am ready to unearth everything around it.

Chapter 7

The Meeting at the Bridge

A deep rusty shade the sky wore that night, as Polly stared outside the cab window. It was crusty and dry and large cracks segmented the vast expanse; the sun lingered longer than usual. As if there was a slight tiff with the moon. Drinking in this anomalous view, Polly sank deeper into her seat. She didn't understand what to expect from this meeting. The shadow of the car elongated on the fairly empty road. The pharmacy they crossed looked packed, so many people ailing and fighting for life. A strong whiff of antiseptic odour filled the car, transporting her to her painful days at the hospital. Someone had freshly painted their fence yellow, the colour shone even with the receding light. On the sidewalk, there were a couple of people jogging. With earphones dug deep inside, they trotted with a determination to fade the universal issues behind the acceleration of their heartbeat.

Given the strange circumstances, Polly couldn't decide whether to inform Jack and Macy about this meeting. What if it was really nothing, should she bother them at this stage, when she herself had no clue, how important or futile it was going to be? The presence of doubt is an innately human feeling. With her fingers pressed absent-mindedly on the keyboard of her phone, she almost dialled Jack's number. Then she simply switched it off and shoved the phone inside her purse and convinced herself not to. She could almost see the bridge now. Just as it came into view, she felt tiny droplets of goosebumps flare on her flesh. She motioned for the cab to stop and paid him before he left. Then she walked down the rickety bridge, as no cars could cross this bridge, as it was ancient and unstable to hold much weight too. She reached the middle and swirled to check behind; her back felt tense, conscious, and uncomfortable. She could almost feel the heat on her shoulders; of someone watching, following, or perhaps targeting her? The night had descended brightly across the sky and the moon and the galaxy of stars became her spectators; whether they were rooting for her or against her she couldn't decide. Under the bridge, was a river—rich cobalt blue in shade, it simmered noiselessly, unobtrusively, meandering deep into the forest. Like a snake slithering, swaying provocatively. This body of liquid had witnessed many deaths and heartbreaks and had been a source of livelihood to the disguised lawbreakers as well as the lawmakers.

It was said the famous eyes of the woods were socketed right at this point, at the centre of this bridge. Polly hurried down the rest of the bridge. It was a good thing she wore her comfortable flats, not her three-inch heels, else she would have certainly tripped and fallen over, she thought to herself. Even though the night had cooled down, a thin misty layer of fog always guarded the woods. Beads of sweat trickled down her back and also a line of it persisted on her upper lip.

The woods were intimidating, even in broad daylight—and more so in the open mouth of the night. As she descended the bridge, she could feel its filthy, clawed fingers stretch out at her, beckoning her with a toothless grin. White, iris-less, vacant, robotic eyes almost pierced her. Violent shudders ran through her body in her own imagination.

She stopped right at the end tip of the bridge, not wanting to tempt whatever was in those woods. Time seemed to drag lethargically, pausing, dozing, and ignoring her completely. Mrs. Smith was nowhere in sight. Polly was cursing herself for even coming down here. What if she had misread the note, what if Mrs. Smith had meant to write something else and had in a hurry written this location? The interim was a plague, spreading across Polly's mind and body, filling her with fear, torment, and sickness.

Every few seconds she turned to look at the other side, slightly jumpy, fidgety, and clammy she felt. She had reached at a quarter to eight, so she was early. After fifteen minutes more she decided, perhaps she should return and confront Mrs. Smith at Baked & Iced. Just as she turned her back towards the forest, she heard prominent footsteps behind her. Finally, Mrs. Smith had come, she thought and tried to turn back. Someone held her from behind, so she wasn't able to turn and look.

"Mrs. Smith! What is this about? Why are you doing this? Please, I beg you, don't hurt me," Polly pleaded. She could smell a strangely odd aftershave; a crisp masculine one with undertones of musk and mint. It was so familiar, she tried to recollect where she had encountered this fragrance. Lost in her dire effort to decipher who this person might be, she didn't realise when a handkerchief filled with chloroform was placed on her nose and a note was slipped into her purse.

When she woke up next, she found herself with a throbbing headache in a cab that had just stopped outside her home. "Who are you? How do you know where I live? Why are you doing all this?" Polly screamed at the driver, jerking his seat.

"Ma'am, please calm down. I am just a cab driver, I was given this address and paid to drop you here. I know nothing else. You have arrived at your destination. Please get off," the driver said nonchalantly.

"You must have seen the person who gave you these instructions. Please describe him or her, anything you remember. This is very important, I will pay you for this information," Polly pleaded with the driver.

"I didn't see his face, he was tall, about six feet or a little less. He had a mask on and he looked particularly strong. I didn't pester him any further, I wanted no trouble for myself. Especially after he had already paid me extra. That's all I can tell you," the driver replied.

"Did you see his eyes, any rings of tattoos on him, limping, or his walking style? Anything distinctive? Please help me."

"Like I said, I wanted no trouble, I have my family to think about too. He looked like trouble for sure."

Distressed, Polly opened the cab door to get out and banged it shut. Occupied with her thoughts, she almost tripped over Jack bending down to lift Macy at the porch.

"Polly, watch out, be careful! Where have you been? I was worried sick about you, I tried your number, but it was switched off. What's going on? Are you alright?" Jack asked, looking worriedly at her.

"I am sorry, Jack, I got caught up at Mrs. Davis's house. We were chatting and didn't realise the time. What's wrong with Macy? Is she all right? She must have been stuck outside because of me. Let's take her inside," Polly said and she unlocked the door while Jack carried Macy inside. She turned to close the door. Something moved in the darkness outside her gate. There was a man standing smoking, wearing a hat and an overcoat, and he was staring at her. She looked at him and felt something cold run down her spine. Just as she made eye contact, he gave her a curt nod and started walking away. She was being watched, followed, warned—what was this about? She trembled as she thought about it. Was her family in danger? Suddenly, she felt very weary, exhausted, and overwhelmed with all the action of the night. As she bolted the door, she went to check on Macy. Jack had just put her down and was about to leave.

Macy tried to wake up and was talking gibberish. Slowly Polly hushed her, covered her with her blanket, and turned on the dim light and air-conditioner. Jack and Polly left the room together, closing the door softly behind them. Outside, Jack tried to coax her into talking again.

"Are you going to tell me what's on your mind? You look pale, P, you need rest, you shouldn't tire yourself out like this. Is there something you want to tell me, let me help you, P?" Jack said.

"No, it's nothing, really, I am just plain exhausted after a long day, I guess. A good night's sleep will do wonders. Don't worry. Let me make something quickly for dinner. You haven't eaten too, I am sure," Polly said.

They had a couple of coleslaw sandwiches and some salad and called it a night. Finally, they retired to bed. Polly couldn't sleep. She kept tossing and turning on her side. She wanted to share her experience, tonight's attack with Jack. But he was already so overburdened, that she didn't have the heart tonight. Perhaps, tomorrow, she could tell him about it. Jack lay awake for longer, a circus of thoughts juggling through his brain. One thing was sure, Polly was not at Mrs. Davis's house, she would never have taken a cab back from there. It was odd that she was lying. He didn't broach the subject, as he expected her to confess whatever was on her mind in the bedroom. Yet she didn't pursue that discussion again. He sighed inwardly and made a silent prayer for the protection of his family. He decided to take the issue at hand more actively from tomorrow morning.

In that very room, there sat an elegant mocha cream-coloured purse with long shoulder straps that lay limp, yawning obnoxiously on either side and the handles were perked up as if any moment they would be ushered into an emergency.

The zipper of the main pocket was interrupted midway through her journey. Perturbed, she stood there rolling her eyes impatiently. Anyone watching her closely would easily see the bag had a lot of pizzazz. Invariably the owner took special care of it always, keeping it clean and not stuffing it till it bulged from all angles like a bald man in his late forties, who had a drinking problem. Yet tonight, this stylish little purse held a secret; one that Polly Mason had not discovered till now. One that perhaps held great power; a piece that fits into this unsolved puzzle in the Mason household, maybe?

Not very far away in the same neighbourhood, someone else was also unable to sleep. The events of the night had transpired way out of proportion. A lady sat in front of the mirror on her dressing table, deep in her thoughts. She was rubbing moisturiser on her skinny hands; the skin had almost turned translucent with a lot of pigmentation and a green web of veins stared back impassively. In the centre of the table, there was a big bottle of baby body lotion—milk and honey tones. On the right there stood a tube of hand cream—chamomile and rose scented, a face moisturising cream, also for babies—mild, paraben-free, hypoallergenic. In the centre drawer, there was a face powder, a couple of half-used, half-broken lipsticks—pale pinks, a hairbrush, and a very old blush, that was almost finished.

She inspected her increasing number of grey hairs on both sides. It made her feel sad. Once she too had been beautiful; she had thick, glossy, brown hair. The wrinkles under her eyes were damp, she had got used to those now. She didn't mind growing old; it was beautiful in its own way. It was rather the new regimen of aches every morning that troubled her, the constant battle was truly exhausting. Although she was much happier lately, her little accomplishment, one that she had yearned for the longest time, had finally come true. She smiled at herself in the mirror, a little victory in her kitty it was. Finally, she went to bed, humming a lullaby, as she brushed away her guilt. She would not let those unpleasant thoughts trouble her tonight; *those can wait for tomorrow surely*, she convinced herself and fell asleep.

Chapter 8

Hallucinations and Medications

Do you remember the night, we lay awake under the sky on our terrace, with our sleeping bags, your olive-green one and my fuchsia pink one? I remember it so clearly, the crisp air—deliciously swirling around us, the sky smooth like a rich black velvet canvas, shimmering with those tiny dots spread over so carelessly; like someone bottled some fireflies and the cap was loose, it broke open and each one of them scattered free. A sweetness I could taste right at the back of my palate, Mama had prepared some sandwiches and your favourite chocolate chip cookies. It was a scarless sky, you said, the moon was nowhere to admonish it; for flaunting her beauty unabashedly. I watched it with my mouth open, hypnotised by the scene and your words.

You whispered into my ear, little Macy, lie awake, let the night rest in you, tonight. Perhaps, it tires too, being a rest for everyone? And so I did, I broke open every dream, and dusted myself off each nightmare that tried to interrupt me. To every crackle, rustle and groan, I listened, waiting for it all to lull, mellow, and mute into a soundless rhythmic snore. This was the most magical experience for a little girl, a five-year-old, created by her ten-year-old brother.

Your endurance has always been your strength as well as weakness. I remember all those times you protected me from Mama and Dad. I did all the mischievous things and you simply spelt them so confidently and they punished you for it. As the years passed by, everyone started noticing the goodness in you. Even in school, you never had any enemies. The only dangerous trait about you was your curiosity, if I may say so. They say it's always good to be curious, yet I have quite a different theory on it. Curiosity is like a magnet, it attracts all kinds of trash around it, drawing trouble and discovery alike, it has no filter really.

I like how I have started talking to you like this, I miss you less, weirdly. Over the last few months, your absence has grown more and more prominent. I used to stop mid-sentence when I suddenly realised I was talking to you and you were not even there. Then, I started talking to you like this; in my head, I can feel your presence almost. I wonder how Mama and Dad cope with your absence? I wish I could share with them, my little clandestine rendezvous with you.

Now, it's time for some investigation. I have the book in my hand, To Kill a Mockingbird. I flip through the pages and ideally find nothing else strange in it. That phrase does not leave me. Chewing my nails, I look at the handwriting again, the letters gawk at me; like I am crazy. It was certainly your handwriting—some of the letters were scribbled—as if in a hurry. Why were you in a hurry, were you afraid of something? Or perhaps of someone? I don't understand. For hours at a stretch, I stared at this strange skeleton of words, unable to connect it to anyone or anything.

Frustrated, I decided something that I never thought I would resort to. It seemed like the sensible thing to do, since I had reached a dead end. Having spent the whole day rummaging through your novels, and finding no other books with any sort of doodle or scribble on it, it only heightened my suspicions. It was time I did something for a breakthrough into this mystery. So, I decided to go to the cops and ask them, plead with them, to open your missing file again. I have no idea if they will agree, yet it was worth the try. Before that though, I needed to involve our parents in this, that's what you would do, I know. I would reveal this piece of information to them after dinner, I decided.

In the living room, I was watching TV. Nothing interested me really. There was a deafening silence in the house, even the scratch of a nail on the wall would sound gut-wrenching. It heightened as the night grew older, accentuating my senses deeply. The clock ticked, water dripped in the kitchen sink, the windows creaked—an odd orchestra this was. I was the lone spectator of this symphony. It was an unending wait; I could sense it—even though I tried to simply ignore it. To distract myself, I climbed out of the sofa and went to prepare some dinner. It was then that I heard the kiss of a stone on a window—which window I couldn't guess. I ran towards my room, but when I opened the door to check—nothing. Then I sprinted to your room and that is when I saw the same window had been shattered and your desk was a mess. It frightened me. I stood paralysed for a few seconds—immobile, uncertain as to what should be done first.

Just as I was about to enter and check the room if anything was missing, I heard the bell. Abandoning the room, I went to open the door. Mama and Dad had returned. I opened the door and started crying, so overwhelmed was I with emotion, I couldn't bring myself to explain to them what the issue was. They tried to calm me down and we sat down in the living room. After Mama made me drink some water, I narrated the incident to them. This piece of news shook them too, it has barely been a few months and another attack like the one on you. Dad called the cops immediately.

By the time the cops arrived, I had just about calmed down. They sat me down and badgered me with a barrel of questions. I was feeling nauseous and petrified; replaying those terrifying events drained me of all my strength. All this chaos made me forget about the phrase altogether.

"What happened, can you tell us exactly what you heard? Where were you? What were you doing?" Chief Grant shot at me.

"I was in the kitchen when I heard a loud shattering sound. As soon as I heard it, I ran to check my room first; nothing was touched there. So, I ran to Jerry's room, and there I saw that same window was broken and his desk was untidy as if someone had rummaged through his books," I described.

"Will you show us the room, where exactly you saw all this?" Chief Grant asked solemnly.

"Sure, let's go, please follow me," I said confidently. The door was open, so I pushed it open and looked at the window and then at the desk. I couldn't believe my eyes. Mama, Dad, and the two officers looked at me for an explanation. I looked at them and back at the room. Desperately I tried to say something—anything rather and found nothing to say.

"How is that possible? I swear I heard the sound and saw what I already told you! Mama, Dad, please believe me," I pleaded, staring back at your room that was spotless and the window also untouched.

The officers spoke to Dad and they finally left. Mama took me to my room and sat down beside me. I was walking in a trance by then. Softly rubbing my back, she tried to comfort me, whispering things that were supposed to make me feel better. I simply stared at the ground and nodded at times. Dad joined her—he was also patiently coaxing me to relax, smile, and untangle. After a while, they decided to leave me alone. Before leaving the room, Mama softly asked me, "Have you been taking your medicine, Mace?"

I don't remember the rest of the conversation, nor do I remember the next few months or so. They simply slipped in and out of my life like my breath—unaware, I just trotted about routine, without giving anything much thought. Talking to you also had become difficult; I simply lost consciousness of what was real and what was really in my head. I was even ostracised at school. It felt like I was drowning in this choking darkness; trusting myself had become an effort too. Tunnels of darkness swept towards me. With my hand stretched out,

I called out soundlessly for help. There was no escape. I tried to grip the threads of wind, and failed, failed, failed unendingly, kicked to attempt a somersault—to rotate myself and see where I was falling. In vain. It became colder as I fell deeper and deeper; I could feel my skin burn, graze, and nip against the jaw of the coldness. The speed was faster, yet it never ended. I felt dizzy, frightened, and disoriented. Every night I diminished inch by inch; what I really wanted, was to disappear completely.

One day, I was staring at the mirror, trying hard to penetrate behind that questioning, defensive, unsure gaze. It was like an out-of-body experience, a version extracted out of me. This strangeness stared at me; sneering at me, belittling me. I cringed and covered my face with my hands. The echoes amplified and faded as if to emphasise my unholy fear. My mouth felt dry and acidic sediment layered all around. A chunk of my inner cheek I had bitten off—my tongue played with that thin layer hanging inside. I was scared, angry, and upset—that everyone saw me, but no one noticed me.

Mama and Dad were trying relentlessly to save what was left of me. They would take me out, buy me ice creams, we would go watch movies. They even bought me tonnes of books on baking, cakes, and pastries, but nothing excited, enticed, or interested me anymore. Losing one child was enough for them. They tried everything not to lose the other one. Sometimes no amount of effort drives in the desired effect, it simply wades, manifesting itself into a tormenting task. Unable to believe anyone or even myself was the shock I was in. Admitting to myself that I might be sick, was I? There were times when I was furious with myself. How could I imagine it? It felt unforgivable.

Chapter 9

Polly's Confession

Jack Mason had a horrible feeling about what was really going on at home. Polly's evasive behaviour was not helping. One day he found her arguing with Mrs. Smith at Baked & Iced. They were always friendly, up until now, and the heated argument was about some covert meeting that they were supposed to have and Mrs. Smith never turned up for it. It was odd that Polly had never mentioned it to Jack. He had just reached the shop on his way back from work when he found them.

"Mrs. Smith, I was waiting there for you at the foot of the bridge and you never came. Your note clearly mentioned the time and place, why didn't you come? You were the one who wanted to meet, it was dark and eerie out there. Still, I waited for you," Polly spoke tight-lipped, gritting her teeth. She didn't think it would be safe or appropriate to mention her strange encounter.

"Polly, my apologies. I was unable to come there myself, so I sent a messenger, didn't you meet with him? Didn't you get the note I sent for you?" Mrs. Smith asked.

"You had sent that monstrous, ill-behaved person? First, he manhandled me, then he covered my face with a handkerchief; I fell unconscious, and he pushed me into a cab and sent me home. I mean who does that? Why would you do that to me? Wait, what note, he gave me no note," Polly sounded exasperated.

"Why, of course, he gave you a note, he has an odd way of working, although he seems to be efficient. Did you check your purse? Now, Polly, I really must go, my customers are getting restless. I only wish well for you, I hope you will understand and forgive me for the trouble I caused," Mrs. Smith held Polly's hand, gave it a brief squeeze, and scurried off.

Jack heard all this standing hidden amidst the crowd near the cash counter. Polly was left standing there alone. She frantically rummaged through her purse and found nothing. Suddenly she realised that this wasn't the bag she had carried that day. So, she left the pastry shop in a hurry. Jack had to go back to work after his lunch break, so he returned to work. His mind was not at ease. Although he had not given up hope on finding Jerry, the chances became slimmer every day. With the police officer's resigned attitude, he just felt like a nuisance going there. Was it possible this would lead somewhere? He was also worried about Macy's delusions. She was so bright, alert, and empathetic always. The loss of a loved one does mysterious things to those attached, he sighed.

Sometimes he wondered about the woods; the eye that legends spoke about. Nothing of this nature had happened in a long time. He had gone to the Central Library and done his research on the same. One of the books—The Woods of Redbarrow—mentioned that centuries back there was a time when every year one child would go missing and never be found again. The people lived in fear; terrorised mothers rocked their children violently to keep them quiet night after night, not sleeping a wink, deep crevices around their eyes, veins protruding out near their wrists. The redness, pain, strain—nothing mattered to the ferocious mother except saving her child. A sweet victory when the night would finally pass. Boys and girls of all ages were swallowed alive. The only form of intimation the town would receive was a shriek; razor sharp, an acrid bitterness in the tone—not so much of pain, more so of shattering despair. An agony so raw, that reading this turned Jack pale like a yellowed sheet of paper. That shriek was what he connected with Jerry's incident.

Polly sat on her bed with her bag upturned on it, the inmates of the bag looking up at her consciously as if woken up from a deep sleep. An assortment of tiny slips of bills which were half crumpled fell out, a bunch of jingling keys, a tiny tube of sanitiser, a squeezy bottle of orange and honey hand moisturiser, a hair brush, a lipstick, an eye pencil, a face powder, a pocket-friendly perfume bottle, and a packet of wipes. Amidst all this, she found a strikingly bright fluorescent green coloured paper—folded twice. She looked at this foreign item, picked it up, and opened it carefully. It smelled strongly of nicotine, and made her cough chokingly. As she finally opened it, there was an odd phrase scribbled on it. It said, "I will return—to me."

She read it over and over again, carefully pulling out the syllables and enunciating each word. She didn't understand what it meant, why did Mrs. Smith send this to her? What did it mean? It absolutely made no sense to her. After reading it a couple of times more, she gave up, folded it carefully, and kept it inside the drawer of her bedside table. It was time to tell Jack about this entire episode, she decided. Mrs. Smith was abrupt, absurd, and mysterious—to understand those words she would have to take Jack's help. Mrs. Smith had said she only meant well for her, what connection did all this have with her, she simply failed to understand.

She worried about Macy. She had become so lost, cold, and aloof all of a sudden after that night's incident. What she really wanted was to discuss this with Macy as well. Mace was always good with this sort of thing. After all, she had grown up watching her Jerry, picking up things from him, listening to him adoringly. How she missed her Jerry! There was a raw ache; gnawing through her resilience—growing wider and wider every single day. It was like her heart had a limp that was simply getting worse day by day. She was a mother; she was not ready to give up yet.

Life measured up at different angles for all of them, yet they had all grown worse, wiser, and wearier altogether. Every scalding sorrow they tried to hide from each other, to prevent adding to the suffering they all knew so well about. Was it possible to live in these cubicles of grief? Polly didn't know, rather was not sure about it anymore. It was distressing really not to be able to share what mattered the most to all three of them. It was time to destress, drown the pain, stifle its persistence and find out, pursue, and conquer the evadingly invasive monster. Even if they had to walk parallel with what might definitively define or damage them forever. Polly Mason would uproot everything to find her son; irrespective of whether he was dead or alive. Now all she needed was to battle up.

Jack returned from work in a pensive mood. He was feeling slightly anxious, on the edge as to what to expect from Polly. When he parked his car on the porch and got out of the car, something caught his attention. There was a man in a black overcoat and a hat, standing across the road, watching his house. This was strange, he had never noticed him before. He almost reached the door, and was about to put the keys inside the lock. He thought, perhaps he should go approach the man and question him. He had just turned around from the door when Polly suddenly opened the door.

"Jack, you are home, come on in. I have prepared dinner, why don't you freshen up and I will set the table. Why do you look so preoccupied? Jack? Come on, let's go," Polly grabbed his arm and pulled him in.

"Nothing, I am fine. Let's go in. Just had a long day at work, I guess. How are you, P? Mm… something smells delicious, is that what I think it is?" Jack turned to close the door and peeped one last time to check on the stranger. Gone!

"Huh! Yes, it is Shepherd's Pie, go on now, I can hear your stomach growling from this far," Polly pushed him in the direction of their bedroom.

Jack smiled to himself in the bedroom. Polly's mood lifted his spirit, he felt less exhausted and more positive to be welcomed home so warmly. All three of them had a nice quiet dinner. Macy talked in monosyllables mostly. She seemed distracted. Jack filled them in with the latest office politics. Polly listened intently and enjoyed a bit of this drama. The sweetness of caramelised cheese, creamy mashed potatoes, and the sizzling minced lamb filled warmth in the house. Dinner ended without any prominent event. Although Jack kept wondering at the back of his mind about confronting Polly about Mrs. Smith, every time he just pushed it away when he saw Macy's sad eyes. He felt helpless, unable to liven her up, all attempts seemed to go astray. Polly offered Macy an extra helping of pie, which she refused politely and continued to play with her food.

Polly got ready for bed after dinner. There was a palpable silence in the bedroom. She sat on her side of the bed and brushed her hair. Jack opened his laptop, put on his reading glasses, and surfed and edited absent-mindedly some presentation for the next day. The silence between them gnawed and bickered skittishly until suddenly both spoke up at the same time and started giggling awkwardly. Jack told Polly to go first. Polly lifted her pillow, unfolded the fluorescent green note, and handed it to Jack.

"What's this, P?" Jack read, frowning at it as if it was written in some foreign language.

"Mrs. Smith sent this for me, Jack. I can't understand what it means at all. I thought you might be able to help. Can you?" Polly asked.

Then she finally spilled the entire episode with Mrs. Smith. She confessed that she had hidden it from him and Macy, as she didn't want to worry them unnecessarily. That she had decided if she found something relevant, then she would share it with them. Now, with this strange note, she thought it was time to discuss it with them.

"I don't understand what these words mean. It is a strange phrase, a message, or perhaps a code. It almost sounds funny; don't you think? Are you sure it's not a joke? Mrs. Smith is known for her pranks, right?" Jack asked. He also confessed how he had overheard them talk at the pastry shop and was feeling hurt that she hadn't confided in him.

"I don't think it is a prank, J. She was behaving quite strangely when she gave me the first note to meet her, like she didn't want anyone to see or know about it. Then, that rough man she sent instead of coming herself. All this doesn't add up funny. What do you think we should do? Should we ask Macy? She is good with de-phrasing such things. Just like Jerry ..." Polly said and stopped abruptly.

"You are right, she is good. No harm in asking her, it will be good to perhaps take her mind off other things. Let me go and check if she's asleep," Jack gently touched Polly's arm and left.

He knocked on Macy's door. No reply. He knocked a couple of times more and then twisted the door knob to open it. He looked around and found nothing. He sprinted to check in Jerry's room. This time he didn't knock and simply barged into the room. He found the lights switched off, but on the bed, sat Macy and she was staring out of the half-open window. A dam of relief exploded and he let out a loud sigh. Macy turned to look at him—uncomprehending, disinterested, dispirited.

"You gave me quite a scare, Mace. I was looking for you in your room and couldn't find you. I see that you are awake. There was something that your Mama and I wanted to ask you about.

We need your help with something. Would you come to our room, please? It might be important—we don't seem to make no head nor tail of it," Jack pleaded, biting his lower lip. Praying she didn't refuse.

"Hmm, sure Dad, I'll just be there. Give me a couple of minutes, I need to visit the washroom and I will join you guys. Is that alright?" Macy asked, guessing this must be one of their tricks to change her mood.

Jack nodded and softly shut the door behind him. After a few minutes, she dragged herself into their room and sat down on the couch. They seemed relieved to see her, Polly smiled at her and walked up to her, rubbed her back gently, and gave her the note. Macy looked at her mother and then read the note.

Book II

Chapter 10

Letters

Dec 22, 1991

Dear Jerry,

At the stroke of dawn, I heard the door mimicking your touch; a soft hollow creaking sound with a tap on the sturdy Mahogany wood. It makes me smile and stir in my sleep; expecting you to tiptoe inside my room and sit on the armchair to watch me asleep. You often told me how you used to love doing that, an unusual tranquillity you found in this. I sink deeper into this velvety slumber – the effect your presence always had on me. Pale yellow sunlight bleaches half my armchair, two of the bedposts, and my dressing table partially, and a beam strikes off the mirror right onto my eyes. Quite a merciless awakener. I frown and pull a soft, tightly stuffed, fluffy pillow over my head—to cover my eyes with it. Then, I remember you.

Pushing away the covers, I sit up to look all around the room, and at last my eyes fall on the undented armchair, sitting all pretty. Damn dreams, I murmur to myself. Every time I wake up from a similar sort of dream, my yearning turns sour and soggy at the same time; like porridge left out of the fridge the night before—unpalatable. Sitting on the edge of the bed, I hit the bed with my back and my head accusingly. The honking, and chirping outside draw a melancholic note. Hunger pangs drag me into the kitchen, where I help myself to slightly burnt toast with some extra cheesy scrambled eggs (although that annoying doctor forbids me from eating cheese). I indulge in it, just to spite him, pamper me, or punish myself perhaps. Thoroughly confused, I feel on the edge. The motive seems to evade me more and more just like you.

The day begins with that all-so-familiar waiting game. I while away time knitting some woollen caps for you. When it gets blatantly cold, you will need them, you know. Then I want to be able to keep you warm. In the study, there is a smell of stale chicken stew and some sharp after tones of permanent markers. Drawing the curtains, I watch a woman jogging in her tracks, holding a Walkman with headphones. The traffic is scanty at this hour, just a couple of cars with fathers dropping their toddlers home from school. It's almost midday.

How are you doing? You must be busy, I assume. I hope you get my letter on time. Now, the postman greets me every time he cycles past me. We share a sad nod. Earlier I used to badger him about your letters. With time, I understood he wouldn't be torturing me of his own will, right? It has been a while since I last saw you. I wish to hear from you at the earliest. Take care of yourself.

I am strong, don't worry about it. Just... nothing.

Blessings and love,
Me.

* * *

April 1, 1993

Dearest Jerry,

The potted plants have withered—Busy Lizzie, Boston Ferns, Coral Beed, and Weeping Fig tree. I don't remember very well if I watered them enough, or perhaps, I did. Why did they die on me, Jerry? It's spring here you know, I remember how you used to love the season of blooming. There was always an extra beat in your walk, you smiled radiantly at everyone. You helped stray animals, bringing them home with you; making me furious. Yet you cared deeply for them and brought them back to life. Does spring greet you there? I guess not, it's mostly remote and cold there and sometimes mercilessly hot. I secretly watched you and enjoyed the way you dedicated your time to old-age homes. Did *you know that? Maybe you did, maybe you didn't. I don't know anymore.*

I cleaned the doormat yesterday; washed it rigorously in a hot soapy solution. Do you remember how you used to like playing with bubbles as a toddler? One day, you were unable to find your favourite duck before your bath and you threw such a tantrum; dragged me to every corner of the house to find it. We did find it in the end! You were uber thrilled; for the next thirty minutes. Near the doormat, I also found a pair of your dirty tennis shoes. I squeezed in some time and managed to give them a good scrub.

Everything around the house screams of you. Your room welcomes me with strong tones of Old Spice aftershave. I hear your bellowing laughter in the damp days, at the groves of darkness. Once a week I prepare your favourite cream of tomato soup, just to be able to taste that incredible glint in your eyes when you slurp it. Day after day I try to envisage your return, but it appears only to fade in fragments, leaving me with a mere figment of my imagination. Sometimes, on certain raw, ruthless days, I sense that you miss me. It doesn't help. It only hurts more.

Your last letter was too brief, do try to write longer and more frequent letters. I am eagerly awaiting your return, so ecstatic about it. Every day I add another dish to the menu. planning to call a gardener to clip the wilderness. I like the wilderness, there is a sort of comfort in it. My hideout when you are not around. There is so much I am planning; I simply want everything to be a surprise.

Blessings and Love,

Me.

* * *

September 25, 1993

Dear Jerry,

You didn't come.

Blessings and Love,

Me.

* * *

September 30, 1993

Dear Jerry,

The officers came today to meet me. I don't believe them. You must come soon now. I am waiting.

Blessings and Love,

Me.

* * *

October 10, 1993

Dear Jerry,

The water is clogged in the kitchen sink. There is leakage in the bathroom, the electricity bills need to be paid. I have stopped taking the newspaper. They spell a lot of lies I cannot digest anymore.

I re-read your last letter, the one you sent in March and you mentioned 'I will return—to me.' I yelled at the postman today, it felt good. This is not good, right? I am scared.

Blessings and love,

Me.

* * *

December 12, 2003

Dear Jerry,

I saw you today. It did something to my heart. The same kindness struck me. The cavern that I am harbouring in for so long, needs rain. Watching you through the window is my favourite hobby now. I call you with an excuse to help me with some fixtures or sell some old books. You smile and always do it so graciously. You don't smell the same though, that's alright, preferences change. In the evenings, I watch you play with the little kids, they are so charmed, besotted, and thrilled by you. I feel myself flush with pride.

Every day, I try to find an excuse to call you over. You come without any qualms—perhaps, simply to help the old lady? When you leave, the hues of the rainbow mute for me, I panic, stutter, and scramble, fearing you won't return.

Something feels odd when you address me so formally, though. How long will you trouble and torment your little old lady, Jerry? I will wait—you must return—like you promised.

Blessings and Love,

Me.

* * *

March 15, 2004.

Dear Jerry,

I found a new way to call you over—to read to me. I was startled to hear you read so well. You were never interested in reading before, yet now, you read like butter sizzles on the pan, accentuating all my senses. It has become increasingly uncomfortable for me not to ask you to stay the night in your own room.

I just want to watch you sleep in your room, and prepare breakfast for you in the morning;

some grilled sausages, hash brown potatoes, and some peanut butter jelly sandwich. Just the way you liked it. Why won't you do that? Come and stay with me. I spend nights planning and plotting, as to how to convince you to stay. You are growing thin; I cannot bear to see that. Your newfound family doesn't give you enough to eat? Or you simply miss my cooking?

Blessings and Love,

Me.

* * *

Chapter 11

Jerry's Dilemma

It was damp, moist, and murky and made him feel as if he was disintegrating. The process was slow; time was let loose at large, like a predator. He was restless, pleading, frightened. Disorientation was high, like an animal left in a cage for an experiment. Someone was watching him, waiting for him to get accustomed to this setup. An attic, he could get that much from stacked up boxes in every corner, a makeshift bed near the almost non-existent window. He was young, smart, and kind; he could surely negotiate, talk some sense into the kidnapper and find his escape out of here. For what had he been kidnapped? His parents were not rich or even famous for that matter. Then why? That's the bit that gnawed at him in the initial few days. He was given food through the narrow opening right at the bottom of the door. No one said anything for days. The food was good, it was tasty, and he was even given generous helpings—a big helping of dessert as well. The food tasted familiar; it was almost on the tip of his tongue. He knew this style of cooking, but couldn't place who though? The soft caramelised fumes sometimes reached him.

The thing with waiting is, memory fades, blurs, and grows fainter and fainter as time passes. It gets so distorted that your imagination overpowers reality. Eventually, there comes a time when you simply can't separate fiction from reality. That's what was happening with Jerry. At first, he was positive, some demands would be made and his parents as well as the police would surely find him and rescue him. He lost count of the days as they grew into bearded months. Hope died a new death at every sunset. He even tried to talk to the person who came to give him food. There was no reply. The rusty-coloured four walls started narrowing in on him. Scratching at his helplessness, at night he heard footsteps and then muffled cackling laughter.

After two months, he developed a routine, like all animals do instinctively for survival. Mornings he would wake up and his breakfast would be already looking at him. He was given some books to read every now and then, so he spent his time reading. Evenings, when the sun melted into the oceanic sphere, he would write on the writing pad he was provided with. He found solace in these two things. He wondered why he was treated well, yet imprisoned like this. It was odd to be stuck like this.

He wept for his family every night. There were no drawstrings to pull anymore. He thought about his little sister Macy, yearned to talk to her, tease her, protect her. Ironically, it was he who needed rescuing now. He thought about Mrs. Davis, the kind lady—an odd parting they had. She was alone and mourning. He didn't want to hold anything against her.

His brown hair had started growing longer. A moustache and beard invaded his face. At times he believed he had hallucinations, out of his desperation to escape. He could hear familiar voices—sometimes it was Macy, then once he heard his mother too. Yet the one he most frequently heard sounded like someone he knew closely. With all the nerve-racking, jittery events going on, he simply couldn't put a finger on it. Strange.

The perpetual lurking paradoxical drone was obtuse. Where would the once forlorn escape? Gallons of sorrow drowned in that attic that seemed less and less like home. Yet, it seemed more and more familiar. Scraped through its languorous mouth, Jerry sat in his loneliness. A pool of sadness was all it took to lose the need for company—in every way he had become what he never thought himself as. A loner, in all its glory and destruction. Inside this solitary confinement, he watched the spider make his web. Intently as it built; picking itself up every time it fell down. What was it about trying that it never gave up? Jerry watched it fascinatedly like a disciple.

Sounds he made were wordless—never were they empty; he nodded his head, shook it, grunted, groaned. Sometimes he found himself laughing just like an exercise to lift off the weight from his chest. Invariably it always ended in an excruciatingly soundless cry. It sucked away every atom of energy, leaving him bereft of emotions.

One night he found his head placed on a lap, soft, warm, and comforting. In his sleep, he wept for what seemed like hours at a stretch. Large thin hands stroked his hair away from his face. Instinctually, he thought it was his mother first—yet it faded as he clearly remembered her soft hands were fuller, and the distinctive citrusy, Sandalwood, and Vanilla notes of her perfume. The smell of a familiar tone of baby lotion sent his memory on a spin. He tried to open his eyes, sit up and look. In vain, his body refused to do either. He heard her sob for him.

What was it like to be free? He soon forgot the taste of it. One whole month he spent romanticising about the crisp air on his face. He would roll, turn and twist his tongue against the grains of the sunlight bubbles that streamed into his room like a triangular prism. To hear the soft crunch of the tires as the newspaper boy passed by. The smell of warm giggling by a couple of school girls crossing the road. He missed his untidy room; clothes lying in a scattered mess everywhere, their family dinners together, sharing secrets with his sister, confiding to his mum about his issues. The taste of Macy's honey brown donuts, that simply melted in his mouth.

It was already six months now.

To him though, it felt longer, as if he knew no outside world. Of late a thought was bothering him, something seemed to fit perfectly and it frightened him. All the signs were pointing towards one person. That last evening of his freedom became more and more prominently etched out. His discovery of those letters, the uncomfortable, bad feeling about that phrase—all seemed to fit in like pieces of a puzzle with his kidnapping, or disappearance, call it what you may. He feared that his guess was correct. Unbelievable as it may seem, it stayed with him for days. Jerry decided to make a plan; to find out if his theory was correct.

As he constructed his plan, he observed the little things about his situation—the food that tasted so familiar, the smell of fresh paint, those frequent visits at nights by this stranger who wept. After giving it much thought, one morning he wrote a small note and tucked it under the dishes on the tray that held his breakfast. He worded it carefully, each sentence cocooning the desperation of his emotions. It read as a calm, reasonable, loving, and sensible suggestion or request. No frills or false exaggeration toned it as needy. He had composed it with delicacy; the fluency of his pretence was unidentifiable. He had understood that this needed to be handled with utmost wisdom and care if he wanted to find a way to get out.

Its time;
To lose, cut, tear,
This separation that lost I,
Of the suffering that it cost Me,
Lands I travelled in just a single pursuit,
Tears that scorched like a bleeding Sun,
How many rainfalls fell short –
Of my yearning that grew anguished?
Relentlessly did I search

And I failed, scathed, bruised,
Resounding my agony of return,
To what did I owe? To find me;
Was I to toil like a farmer?
Or fight like a soldier?
Perhaps, beg like a deranged beggar?
Yet. I dragged on, through each trial,
The strings of return did I hold on to tight,
Oh! I see it now, the window of return,
Me, standing there peering at I;
Closer it looks, then the minute gone by,
Clearer I see the shade of my attainment,
Me—my mother; do take me in your embrace,
I have returned—To Me.

Tucked tightly under the dishes, it left his attic. He waited twitchily for a reaction, a response. Lunch went by without a sign. He got two pieces of roast chicken and a generous portion of mashed potatoes with warm buns and some greens. Nothing about the note he heard. He felt betrayed, as if he had failed an examination—for which he had been preparing for so long. Sinking, that was what he was experiencing, quicksand so strong he couldn't hold on any longer. It was not yet evening—darkness invaded him violently. Once upon a time, he had felt comfortable in darkness. Now after his abduction, it filled him with uncertainty— the uncertainty of being attacked. The shock of it was unnerving even after so long.

What happened to the note, he wondered? Did it get thrown into the trash bin? Or did it get washed away down the sink? He simply couldn't fathom. Was it possible that his theory was all wrong, was someone else behind this? What if she did read it and simply ignored his note, perhaps didn't even trust his intentions? Whatever the reason may be, he didn't get the reaction he had expected. He was not ready to send another note yet. It didn't seem like a clever idea anymore. He would have to plan with more precision.

That night the note had found its way—tucked safely under a pillow that was drenched with happy tears after a very long time.

Evening droned, quaked, and sat across the sky almost bored. Through the tiny window, he gazed outside, absent-mindedly. Its expanse was filled with froth, like something was cooking up there —to the point of curdling; no one was watching. Jerry waited for it to spill over, staring at it as it caught his attention. Almost as if he was willing for it to crack open and one star would mistakenly fall into his window. With one of the sharp edges of the star, he wanted to unwind time to the day he got kidnapped, and erase, scratch out, scrub this episode out altogether. Then, he would simply tie up the ends—as if nothing had gone astray and his life would run on a regular course of action. Happy.

He heard the door banging, someone screamed—it sounded like his mother.

"Open the door, let me in, my Jerry is in there!" Polly kept screaming the same line over and over again.

"Mama, you came, thank God. It's okay, wait, I will open the door, just give me a minute," Jerry replied.

He scrambled off his covers, ran towards the door, and turned the knob. It was too tight. With all his might he pulled it. In vain. It didn't budge. On the contrary, it got tighter. Polly kept screaming and banging as if she couldn't hear him.

Jerry was perspiring heavily, his heartbeat accelerated rapidly. A strange animalistic sound came from inside him—something between a cry and a roar. He decided to break the door and looked all around for anything to bang it with. The chair shattered against the door. He rummaged through the dusty old boxes in the attic. There he found a hammer; he couldn't believe his luck. He ran towards the door and lifted it to bang the door. Just as he was about to bang it, letters started raining on him heavily. The screaming increased a pitch higher and he could hear someone cackling too. The chaos was only getting larger. In between all this, he could taste blood—salty, metallic. There was blood all over the wooden flooring; several disturbing cuts on his body were gawking at him. He felt weak and dizzy and panicked. Thud! He fell off his bed.

Chapter 12

Officer Scott's College Visit

Police officers Grant and Scott were in the middle of an intense discussion; it was late at night. They were supposed to return home about two hours back. Yet, here they were, working overtime. The thing about these two cops was that they never did give up easily. Even though the world at large thought the case of that missing boy, Jerry Mason was closed, in reality, it was very much in progress. They had been keeping close tabs on the immediate family and the neighbours as well. The family was not taken into confidence as yet, as they feared those compromised might get alerted.

Chief Grant had noticed the recent irregularities in their behaviour, the mother's visit to the woods. He had sent a couple of cops in casuals to follow her, and see what this meeting was about. Unfortunately, they missed the few seconds when she was shoved inside the cab. The sister's hallucinations and the all-too-simple father. He had his doubts about all of them, about the motive— they all seemed to have a little bit according to him.

"The events are not adding up, they seem to be getting odder by the day," Chief Grant whispered almost, easing the frown lines on his forehead with his fingers.

"Chief, the thing which is most baffling, is that all the three events are isolated, no link, or connection to each other," Officer Scott pondered and stated.

"Indeed, something strange is going on, we need to move in closer, tighten the boundaries. Scott, first thing tomorrow, I want you to check on the sister. I have a hunch, she will lead us somewhere. I know I don't need to tell you to be discreet. Just don't raise any alarm, it's not time yet," Chief Grant added.

"On it Chief, first thing tomorrow morning. I will go down and do it as inconspicuously as possible. I was thinking, we should tap all their phones, we might find some clue, perhaps?" Officer Scott suggested.

"Hmm... alright, do that. No harm in trying. It has already been six months, what do you think Scott, is it worth the chase?" Chief Grant found himself asking.

"No, I certainly think so, we are surely getting warmer, I can feel it. Plus, we have never been known to give up a case, right, Chief?" Officer Simon Scott said giving a boyish grin. Grant smiled back looking more reassured, although the question was more rhetorical than anything else.

"What about the neighbours? Did you get anything out of them? Anything they might have seen and found strange perhaps? I am sure someone had to see something, that they are finally ready to reveal after so many months have passed by," inquired Grant.

"We did interview each and everyone around that neighbourhood, yet that was a long time back. Maybe I could send a couple of officers to question them again, now?" Scott said thoughtfully.

"Do that, talk to the teachers and friends at school too, again. No harm in that, as well. Just spread out as wide as possible. A boy has disappeared and we aren't able to locate him. It is a disgrace, really. No ransom demands, no body found, something strange is going on in Redbarrow Woods and I don't like it at all. I can feel it, Scott. We need to get to the bottom of it," grunted Chief Grant.

"Sure, sir," Scott assured.

"Let's call it a night, it's late. Come home for dinner. Susan and the kids will be happy," Grant ordered.

"Not tonight, sir, maybe another night. It's already late, you should spend time with them," Scott smiled pleadingly.

"Scott, I didn't ask you, I am ordering you. Come on now, let's get out of here," Grant said.

They had been working together for over ten years now. Together they had solved many mysteries. Over time their bond had become stronger. Officer Scott being younger in experience and age, respected Grant to the point of worshipping him. He admired how sharp he was and how he sacrificed his family life for the job. It was pure passion. He felt bad for his family, though, and that was one of the reasons he had never got married. He didn't want his wife or children to suffer on account of his job, passion, or whatever this had become to him.

Grant treated him like his younger brother. He invited him home for dinners, Christmas, and Easter. His wife and kids were fond of him too; over the years he had become like family to them. His wife often tried to set him up, urging him to get married and start his own family. In vain. He never had any long-lasting relationships.

Scott realised this case was easily relatable to Chief Grant, it was something that could happen to his own sons, David and George. David was studying in the same batch as Jerry. Although he had found out recently, they were not close, mere batchmates. Still, it must be unnerving for him to even think about such a thing as a father.

The night crawled, prowled, and snarled around quietly as they finally drove through the neighbourhood. The light flickered in the lamp post outside the Mason household. A black cat eyed them as they zoomed past Baked & Iced, scratching her back against the corner of the wall. The roads shone bright like a velvet carpet freshly unfurled for the night. Abandoned. The wind crackled, a slight shiver licked the skin, and the cloudless sky seemed parched. A routine howl from the woods greeted them as they passed by. Inside the car, the silence yawned shamelessly, widely, and lazily. The car had a strong scent of cigarettes, mixed with the delicate tones of stale perfume and sour sweat notes.

Both seemed deep in thought, far away from the city of Redbarrow. The weather has a way of tempting the mind to escape the body and wander like a stranger to stray. Orphan memories—clinging to that soft flannel last hug, that unmade bed weighing heavy with a wreath of half-eaten confessions, the eyes of death pleading, un-pleading to be found, to be left alone perhaps. So much closer home they were, yet life, driven off to that cliff, finds no return. Circling around aimlessly on acceleration, what the heart really fears, is the brakes that try to seduce them to stop. There is no end really until you actually taste the end.

Not very far away a mother sleeps, mumbling prayers for a lost child. A husband squeezes his eyes tight, only to stop his guilt from consuming his sanity completely. A neighbour coughs loudly as if admonishing the nightmare to fade. A young girl creeps soundlessly out of bed—slides open the window and jumps out of it. A bottle pops open, cackling laughter dries up, and an attic sits uncomfortable and grim.

The next morning Officer Scott chalked out his plan for the day. After returning from Grant's house, he had a restless night. The last discussion at work had settled somewhere in his subconscious and warped images and thoughts invaded his normally peaceful sleep. He decided to start with the college first thing in the morning.

Mr. Peter Jones, the Principal, was a middle-aged man, a true disciplinarian. For generations, his family had been part of the school, as board members, and Principals as well. Slightly bald, he had a lean framework, and the aura around him exuded immense inspiration. Perhaps, it was something about his deep voice and the way he weighed and pronounced each syllable that created that impact.

"Officer Scott, please sit down, how can I help you today?" Mr. Jones screened Scott from top to bottom.

"Mr. Jones, I just had a couple of questions more on the Mason kid's disappearance. Simply rechecking if I might have missed anything the last time, that could help us track him down," Officer Scott explained.

"Jeremy Mason was a good lad; he was one of the brightest students. It came as a shock to us as well—his disappearance. He was not the mischievous kind, mostly kept to himself, always helping others. Contrary to popular belief, his peers always looked up to him, and sought his help as well as advice. The teachers were fond of him too; his grades were excellent. The last day he had come to school, was also a regular day, nothing unusual had happened. As I mentioned earlier, we are more than happy to cooperate with the police to help in any way we can. Yet as of now, that is really all I can help you with," Mr. Jones said dismissively.

"Is there anyone he was close to, who could have picked up some hint, of what was going on with him perhaps? Mrs. Polly Mason said after he returned from school that particular day, he seemed disturbed and had a few cuts and bruises on his arms," Scott enquired.

"You can check the CCTV footage; from school, he had returned unharmed. Ms. Mary Murphy, his English teacher was the closest to him. Since he was pursuing to be a writer, he took extra classes with her. I am sure you have questioned her earlier, plus she is on leave right now, and will be back in two weeks. Now, if you will excuse me, I have another meeting, Officer," Mr. Jones smiled curtly, standing up and extending his hands.

"Can I get her address perhaps? Ms. Mary's? I won't take up any more of your precious time. You have a good day, sir," Scott stood up to leave after taking down the details.

Outside the campus, the sweltering hot sun received Officer Scott devilishly. Frowning at the piece of paper, he put it inside his pocket, making a mental note to visit her later in the day. The traffic at this hour seemed oddly busy. On his way to the Masons' household, his stomach grumbled, feeling deprived. He parked his motorcycle near Baked & Iced and decided to pamper his tummy a bit, knowing pretty well, if he didn't eat, his analytical skills as well as observation power would flicker unholy. The smell of sweet, freshly baked croissants almost made him dizzy; he wondered how this tiny eatery was always buzzing. Then, the first bite into his Pizza Margarita gorged away all such questions. After finishing his meal, he smiled and nodded at Mrs. Smith, and left.

On his way, he found himself thinking about the case again, going over the details. On the other side of the road, a girl wearing a hood raced past him on a bicycle. He reached the Masons' household and rang the bell. No answer. He rang it twice more and still got no answer. From another window, someone watched him carefully, contemplating, pondering over the reason for this visit. Not liking it one bit, the idea of this unexpected intrusion in the neighbourhood. Officer Scott groaned and kicked the wall. How he hated a futile journey! It was like getting stuck at a roadblock on a long expedition. He decided to wait ten minutes more and then go down to Ms. Murphy's place. This visit was supposed to look like a casual one, hence he decided against calling up and asking the Masons' whereabouts. After waiting for about half an hour, Officer Scott decided to end this tryst and ventured out towards Ms. Mary's place. Even though he knew she wouldn't be there, he still wanted to try his luck, perhaps snoop around the house of this person Jerry Mason was close to.

Chapter 13

A Body in the Woods

June 29, 2004

Dear Jerry,

All my letters have been returned to me since the thirtieth of September nineteen ninety-three. I am so furious with this glitch from the mailing department. How can they say such things? Incorrigible, atrocious, and absurd they are. So, I have decided to change to a private mail service. They will probably charge me more; I don't know how I can afford that. Let me find an alternative.

I am growing ever so fond of you—I hope you end this game soon. My yearning grows unbearable. Sometimes, there is a vacant look in your eyes; when I sort of pamper you with presents or your favourite food. You don't like them; you gulp it down, I notice, so I don't feel bad. Strange. Your brown eyes grow darker when you're uncomfortable, did you know that? I noticed it recently. You keep your hair slightly longer now, and have started growing a stubble too. I like you in this new look too. All I want to do is save you from the big bad world out there. Embrace you away from sadness and fear.

The other day, you did a fresh coat of paint in my room. The shade you chose is brighter than the last one. A brighter shade of blue—sea green colour. You always did love the heady plastic smell of fresh paint. That day you stayed a little longer. It made the colour red in my veins slightly thicker and brighter. It even flowed more smoothly from my brain to my toes. No, really it did. It is becoming more difficult to let you go.

Blessings and Love,

Me.

* * *

November 14, 2004.

Dear Jerry,

I can't take it any longer. It's time. I have everything planned in detail. You know I will always protect you. My pleading eyes, perhaps, fall short in convincing you. The ache grows stronger every day and so does the restless monster inside.

Blessings and Love,

Me.

* * *

January 15, 2005.

Dear Jerry,

You found my letters last evening; this is what I always wanted. Yet, this should not have happened this way. I watched you read them, hiding behind the door. You panicked. There was fear and tears in your eyes. This is not what I had planned. At least not how I planned for you to find out. You ran away in a hurry; I didn't stop you nor did I broach the topic.

It's time. I have arranged for everything. It will all go smoothly.

Blessings and Love,

Me.

* * *

February 25, 2005

Dear Jerry,

I am finally at peace. Everything has gone just as I had planned. At first, I was slightly scared; that things might go wrong. There was a lot of risk at hand. I found a shadow; a person who was swift, confident, and ruthless in his work. Earlier on, I was slightly sceptical about him, about the deed itself too—he made it sound quite simple. I guess he is used to this sort of work—with the kind of money he demands.

Terrible thoughts ran through my mind. What if something goes wrong? What if he hurts you? I wouldn't be able to bear it! I hid in my study cubicle, crouched on the chair, lights dimmed, pretending to be as normal as possible. My fingers felt cold, brittle, and reluctant. For a while, I simply paced around like a caged animal. Then turned to peep outside the window. The street was barren of life. The air was impregnated with a shrieking silence. The monstrosity of the interim was staring back at me with big round eyes.

Then, the event fell off, crashing like dominoes, one after the other. Grinding my teeth together I waited; in the process, I almost bit off a chunk of my lower lip. The blood tasted salty, and oddly I relished it. Now that I think about it, it makes me shudder, a delirious laughter plays at the back of my mind. At the pure ecstasy of this seamless success. Now, it's time to celebrate, time to end my letters to you.

Our time has finally arrived, Jerry.

Blessings and Love,

* * *

There it was by the beach, a quaint cottage. Even from a distance, Officer Scott could see how the soft waves fussed, flirted, and fortified this little cottage. As he drew closer, dusk was sailing across the sea flamboyantly. That rusty hue across the sky gave an almost royal tinge to the whole mood. On the verandah, he noticed lampshades being lit up by an old lady. She didn't notice him watching her, humming a soft tune to herself as she waddled around. Scott assumed she must be Ms. Murphy's mother or aunt. She was not very tall, had an oval face, big round inquisitive eyes, and was warmly plump. The most striking feature was her auburn hair—even with the roots fading grey, it complimented her, even from far he could make that out.

"Good evening, Miss, I am Officer Scott. Such a lovely evening. I hope I am not disturbing you; you look almost angelic against this beautiful scenery," Officer Scott found himself complimenting the lady and his ears turned slightly pink.

"Oh! I didn't notice you there, Officer. Aren't you a kind soul to compliment this old lass? You almost gave me a heart attack. I must be becoming deaf. Please come in," the old lady said.

"My apologies, I should have announced more subtly perhaps. I am here regarding a missing boy. Jerry Mason—he is a student at the same school as Ms. Murphy teaches. The Principal gave me this address. I believe she is on a holiday. I wanted to meet with her. Do you know when she will be back?" Scott asked.

"Well, you are in luck, Officer Scott. She has returned from her holiday, just today. I have nothing to say about Jerry Mason. I already told the other officers all I knew six months back," Ms. Murphy said with tears filling her eyes.

"You are Ms. Murphy? Oh, I am sorry, I didn't know."

"What, you thought I was too old to be Ms. Murphy and you were expecting someone younger and prettier? I get that all the time," Ms. Murphy took off her glasses to rub her eyes.

"No, not at all. My apologies once again. Ms. Murphy, please do let me start over again. I don't mean to antagonise you at all. I can see that you care about Jerry, you are upset that the system has closed his file and is doing nothing about it. Actually, we have not closed the case, we are just doing it more discreetly. You can rest assured we will do our best to find him," Scott said.

"I will be more than happy to talk about Jerry Mason. Such a darling boy he was, always warm, helpful, and courteous. I cannot imagine such a thing could happen to him. You know he didn't have any enemies, at least not in school. The last day, after class, he came to me—telling me excitedly how he had enjoyed the last lesson so much. I still remember his eyes. You know, only very few people have eyes that reflect their soul in them. He was the latter kind," Ms. Murphy said, and smiled remembering him.

She went inside to bring a tray with two cups of tea and some cake and offered them to Officer Scott. She looked more relaxed after his reassurance.

"Did you notice in the last few days before his disappearance any unusual behaviour? Was he worried about something, planning something perhaps? Anything at all out of the ordinary?" Officer Scott asked, sipping his tea.

"He was normal; he didn't seem disturbed or anything. He seemed preoccupied, he was spending his free time with someone. I am sorry I don't know who, I didn't really ask him. I didn't think it was my business to pry into his personal life. Simply because it made him happy. Now when I think about it, I just wish… wish I had paid more attention. This could be completely irrelevant really," Ms. Murphy sniffed back her tears, and offered him some more cake.

"Please don't apologise, any information could come in handy. You never know what would finally break the case. Thank you very much for your time. If there is anything else you remember, please don't hesitate to give me a call at any time of the day or night." Officer Scott shared his card and left.

After a fairly exhausting day, Officer Scott returned to the Police Station. The sky had turned a shade of lilac, as if the heavens above were in a brooding, slightly wistful mood. It seemed as if noon and dusk had a clandestine affair and the time zones had mellowed, blurred, and united. Everything on the road, exposed to the expanse of the sky turned slightly tepid, slow, and arched with a lazy drawl. Bereft of any zing, Officer Scott entered to attend the evening debrief with his team. Even inside, the mood seemed damp. Primarily it had got heightened by the unproductive day that had gone by. Chief Grant asked Scott to stay back after the meeting.

Shuffling some papers on his desk, Chief Grant quietly listened to Scott as he shared the result and progress of his interrogations. Scott also shared with him that he didn't find anyone at the Masons' household. So, he would have to go there again tomorrow.

"There is one more thing I observed and wanted to share with you, Chief. Ms. Murphy knows something, something she's holding back, perhaps she is frightened. I don't know. The reason I didn't pursue it was that she might close up completely. I need to win her confidence so she doesn't hesitate in confiding in me," Officer Scott explained.

"You do what you need to, to get that information out. Finish off with the Masons tomorrow, find out if they have anything, and let them know we are working on the case and that any help from them would help us. Do you need me to come with you?" Chief Grant asked.

"No, not yet, I will meet with them tomorrow and let you know if there is anything important. I think tomorrow I can also meet with the Smiths—the Baked & Iced owners, and a couple of other neighbours," Officer Scott replied.

Chief Grant nodded and they were about to leave for the day, when the phone rang. Scott answered the call, and his face contorted, looked stricken, and went pale. Finally, when he hung up, his voice came out like a hiss. Chief Grant stared at him with an impatient, questioning gaze. When Scott found his voice again, he repeated.

"They found a body."

Chapter 14

Identification of the Body

Blank. That's how I felt at first. Immediately, I was transported to a bone sawing machine. There was a bulky, hairy man holding my limbs expertly together, slicing me slowly limb by limb. I jumped out of it, just as he was about to pass that blade through my neck. I was not able to look at words anymore, yet the words stared back at me.

That same phrase that had almost destroyed me, pushed me back to sanity. I don't know why; I simply couldn't look at my parents watching me read this. The silence swayed, pricked, and bled ruthlessly. I gulped dollops of saliva, there was barely any left in my mouth. They were patient with me, I don't know what reaction they were expecting—they didn't push me an ounce.

Yes, I did take my time. I read it again and again just to make sure I was not hallucinating this as well. Once I confirmed this was the same phrase, I wanted to scream and tell them everything about how I had discovered it. That was a moment of weakness. In reality, though, I found myself simply sitting there calmly, reading it, then folding the pink sticky note and giving it back to Mama. Now, I was contemplating where I should begin.

If there was a beginning at all, I couldn't find it. it felt like I was right in the middle of a pool of letters that frightened, intimidated, and confused me. Not good. Clearing my throat, I was suddenly excruciatingly thirsty. I willed myself to get up and walk out of the bedroom—leaving them staring at me. I thought I heard a unanimous sigh from there, as if they were holding their breath for my reaction, and I simply left. Into the kitchen I walked, drank some water, and decided it was time to rescue them from their dilemma—to thaw the ice that was piercing them so hard. First, I wanted some answers.

When I entered the room again, they were sitting there—yet they looked far away. As if uncertainty somehow was strangling them softly, and they seemed so terribly lost on the wheel of hope. Dad had a worn-out look on his face, Mama was biting her lower lip—clutching the pink chequered bedsheet tightly with her two hands. Both stared at me, unsmilingly. Everything looked shades of pink somehow. The light beaming out of the bedside lampshade looked fuchsia, Mama's handbag had a hue of bubblegum, and the cushion on the couch looked tinted strawberry pink. Every hue arrested me blindly and gave me a throbbing headache. I began my interrogation.

"Where did you find this note, Mama?" I asked quietly.

"Mrs. Smith sent it for me. You don't look surprised to see it, Mace, have you ever seen this before?" She said and continued to narrate her part of the story.

"Yes, I found one a few weeks back, that same phrase was written on the book Jerry was reading right before he went missing." I found myself telling her more than I intended to, which was unlike me. "I tried to investigate a little, but found nothing. I was planning to share it with you both, discuss it with you, and that night itself that incident happened in Jerry's room," I elaborated. Somehow, I found myself feeling lighter almost after sharing this with them.

"Oh, honey! I wish you would have told us about all this," Dad spoke up and hugged me.

Until then, I didn't realise how much I needed that hug. A thunderous crash it evoked in me and I started whimpering like a kitten—sheltering in his hug. There was an explosion inside me, and I withheld absolutely nothing. Then, once again a thickness loomed in the air—anxiety, fear, a deafening dread. That one ghastly question that canopied over us all. What if something bad had happened to you? To our Jeremy, what if this was the very clue, crying at us and we never noticed or perhaps simply ignored it for too long? Most pertinent one being, what if it was simply too late?

Suddenly we found ourselves all huddled closer together. Slightly jittery, unsure, afraid. It was late at night. Even with the air-conditioning on, we were sweating. Dad said first thing in the morning we must inform the police about it. How and when we all fell asleep, I can't seem to recall at all. In the middle of the night, we all woke up in different corners of the same room. It felt as if we were in our own personal jails—of guilt, grief, and fear.

It was about two o'clock when the bell rang. I ran to answer the doorbell. I was surprised to see Officer Scott (at least I think that was his name) standing outside. At first, I felt terribly afraid, that he was the bearer of some bad news—my fingers fumbled at the latch, but finally, I managed to open it. My eyes bored into him like a laser, and he flinched inwardly.

"Is your father home?" He asked meekly, apology oozing out of him. I nodded and ushered him inside.

"Officer Scott, what a coincidence! I was actually just about to visit you at the station. Is something the matter?" Dad questioned. I knew he could feel it too.

"Mr. Mason, there was a body discovered a few hours back in the woods. I need you to come with me to identify it, please. My team is already there, we need to leave immediately," Officer Scott added.

"A body, what do you mean, I need to identify it? Are you implying what I think you are?" Dad asked with some effort. He ran his fingers through his combed curly hair.

Mother started whimpering and ran towards the washroom. This was it. Was this it? I couldn't breathe; the air simply refused to pump into my lungs. Now, why now? I wanted to scream. I felt an unusual force pushing me to shove this man outside the door and slam him shut and erase all that he had ever said. Various versions of violence played in my head—I wanted to hit his head repetitively against the wall, until no one would ever recognise him. Perhaps, I could simply set him on fire, his cries would extinguish the pain I was feeling. In reality, all I did was stare at him frozen, immobile, pale.

Dad was on his way out with the officer when Mama and I ran to plead with him not to leave us in this distraught state—to take us with him. Reluctantly, he did agree and we followed in our car, while he left in the police car.

That journey was the longest one I had ever been in. Even though it was hardly a thirty minutes drive to the woods, it felt strangely long. The sounds accentuated in irregular rhythm, the clanking, constant honking of heavy-duty trucks carrying logs that passed by, the woof of the stray dog, and the meow of the pet kitten. All of it felt as if they were attacking, badgering, and drilling over me. Mother sat there beside me, while I was driving—she was only there physically. There was a lot of traffic, as the trucks were permitted to transport goods only post-midnight—to curb traffic jams during the day.

The russet ripples in the sky looked like they were skipping, flipping, looping through our destinies. The clouds were impregnated with secrets, storms, and confessions. It was the time for a change of season—they would no longer hold back. I could already smell the petrichor in the air; from the right drizzle, it was clear an explosion of rain was due. Bolts of lightning, and resounding thunder loomed, and the howling wind sounded sorrowful and slightly like an opera. Was the mood setting in for a revelation? I couldn't fathom what news awaited us. My clammy hands wrung the steering wheel more tightly. We were getting close to the location. The gushing rain and its orchestra gave little or no hope to our spirits. Mother was getting restless in her seat. Even I didn't have the courage or spirit to do small talk and lift her soaked, drenched fears.

The police car in front was slowing down. I noticed we had come right up to the middle of the forest. Nothing was visible or very clear. The woods today seemed gloomier than I could remember. It was as if every hue of green had decided to mark its attendance here. The timeless, ancient pine trees soared right into the lightning-filled skies. The branches were entwined somewhere in between, like they were related, and clung to each other through storms or even excavations. Do you remember how much I enjoyed playing in the woods with you? I could almost feel the smoothness of the bark on my palms. Running around, giggling with anticipation here as the crisp wind playfully caressed the leaves. The ground was wet, slippery, and damp. Shrivelled up leaves were half trampled into it.

Soft rustling leaves weighed down, drooping with millions of raindrops. The usual scurry of squirrels, birds chirping calling out to their kin, and the rodents scampering along softly through the foliage were all missing. Except for the occasional hummingbird's shrill wing whistle, it was hauntingly vacant. This was not silence; it was simply vacant. Like every living being was holding its breath, choking back the most excruciating screech riding up its throat viciously. The sweet smell of swampy earth filled my senses.

Up ahead a few steps away, as we got out of the car, I saw the yellow caution tag all around the trees—of a crime scene under investigation. Police officers were doing their business, taking notes, finding clues, collecting samples—anything to build a case against or for the deceased. They had set up some portable lamps to light up the place. A bunch of reporters looked at the scene hungrily, like scavengers waiting to snatch and tear into their bite of the story. This scene struck me somewhere deep in the gut. It made me realise one thing. We may not all be related in life, yet in death, we are all related. In more ways than one, we are all related in death. In what way, you ask? Well, for starters, life enlarges the differences—struggle, fame, and fortitude become like a never-ending irregular graph and we are always sprinting in this marathon to reach. To reach where, I have no idea. The end? Whether we sprint, jog, take long strides or perhaps simply sit or sleep—we will anyway reach there, right? The end—death. Where we are stripped of every atom that made us feel glorious or majestic. We will be shrouded in that crisp white cloth—buried or cremated as you prefer it. Levelled—related, right?

We struggled to reach up to where the body was kept. Dad got VIP escorting through the crowd. Somewhere in this chaos, we were forgotten, or perhaps purposely not remembered. I held mother's hand, pushed people, and made our way in front. A potpourri of sweat, smokes, and stale deodorant pinched through my senses. Camera flashes blinded us from seeing too far ahead. The animals must have sensed this invasion in their territory, survival instincts were vigilant and they steered off our course. I could see Dad now; he was standing there immobile. I couldn't read his expression clearly. He looked puzzled, petrified, and something else, I don't know what that was.

We reached closer, from where we could see the body. I was desperate now, to identify and finally dunk into a definitive conclusion. I saw the body at the same time as Mama, and just as I held back my reaction, she squeezed my arm tightly and turned away her face. I couldn't look away. I felt ravenous—an itch at the back of my mind grew stronger. I abhorred looking at it, yet I simply couldn't stop. My brain refused to process an answer. Was I confused? No, I was definite.

Chapter 15

Mrs. Smith Denies

Baked & Iced was getting prepped up for the season of celebration—the year's end. There were many elaborate menus, new dishes, and attractive gift hampers planned. There was a tinkle in the air. Just as someone entered the pastry shop, they could feel pixie dust being sprinkled on them. The smell of warm croissants—butter melting and cinnamon warmly crusting over it wafted softly, caressing the lonely souls that arrived in the early hours of dawn.

The sky had a feathery texture—a million clouds canvassed around slightly quivering. No rains taunted the breaking dawn. The wind in her seductive mood lulled, shushed, teased. Mrs. Smith walked out of her pastry shop to talk to her supplier about the new list of supplies needed. Almost immediately she rubbed her hands against her arms—feeling the chill. The stains of coffee on her palate turned slightly bitter. Twirling her tongue over it, she tried to draw warmth from it.

Her mind wandered to that abandoned boy in the woods. She shuddered at the thought of her own son of the same age lying in the woods like that. Disfigured head—as if a rock had bashed it up several times, the limbs were intact, yet with various cuts and bruises, it said in today's morning newspaper. How could someone be so ruthless, she wondered? Of course, they wouldn't be in the right state of mind. Rage has an arrogant way of getting things done. The supplier was compelled to repeat everything twice for a confirmation as her mind seemed far away.

Just as she finished with the supplier, she was beckoned inside the shop by one of her employee boys. He said, “Ms. Smith, some Officer Scott has come to see you. What should I tell him?”

“I’ll be there in five minutes, tell him to make himself comfortable, please,” Mrs. Smith suggested. She guessed it had to do about the murder last night. After she sent the supplier back, she hurried back inside.

Baked & Iced was buzzing with people now, like bees come to collect honey perhaps. She smiled at her regular customers and scanned the lot looking for an officer in a uniform. He stood at the far end of the pastry shop talking to an old man, who in her opinion simply talked too much. He seemed to have an opinion about everything—yet he barely said anything positive about anyone. She rolled her eyes and slid between the crowds, moving towards the officer. The officer in her opinion looked young. How much experience he had or how efficient he was at his work was hard to tell from his boyish looks. Just as she mentally assessed him, instinctively he caught her eye. Officer Scott realised who it was and nodded his head dismissively at the old man and waited for Mrs. Smith.

He found a motherly warmth in her eyes. He could easily understand how she attracted people to trust her easily. There was something sharp, alert, and focused about the way she observed things. Instinctively, Scott had a feeling she might be able to give him a piece of information that might help crack this case.

“Mrs. Smith, it is a pleasure to meet you. What a lovely place you have got here. Everything looks delicious on the counter and absolutely everyone has only nice things to say about the smorgasbord of delights you offer here,” Officer Scott grinned.

"It's the love of the people here, that brings out the warm essence in the dishes we cater to them. Thank you for your appreciation. Although, I am fairly sure, you didn't merely come here to taste some dessert or praise me. Tell me, Officer, how can I help you?" Mrs. Smith said with a slight glint of inquisitiveness in her eyes.

"Well, I have to admit, you are right about that bit. As you would have heard, we are investigating the case of Jerry Mason. With the recent developments in the case last night, it has further become more intense. I am actually interviewing everyone in the neighbourhood—any information that you may have and have not yet shared with us, might be vital, helpful to us," Scott explained.

"To be honest, last night's events were quite unnerving. I cannot even fathom, what the family of the deceased must be going through. So gruesome, gory, and glaringly evil, this kind of thing has never happened in Redbarrow Woods, as far as I can remember. I wish I could help you with any information that could help. My apologies, though, there is nothing I know that the police don't already know," Mrs. Smith stated quite plainly, not meeting his gaze.

"I see. Just in case you do remember or hear from anyone about anything suspicious, please do feel free to give me a call any time of the day or night. And Mrs. Smith, you don't need to be afraid of anyone. I will ensure nothing gets linked back to you. Think about it, what if this was your own son, would you still say the same thing? I will take your leave now. You have my card. Anytime, I mean it." Officer Scott lifted his hat, nodded, and walked out.

From the way she didn't meet his gaze while answering, he felt certain, she knew something and was frightened to share it at present. So, he played it delicately and let her take her time, slipping his number to her. They eventually come around, his experience nudged.

Mrs. Smith stayed put where she was standing, a shiver running down her spine. She sighed heavily, suddenly feeling very weary and aged. She wanted to tell the officer, but somehow, found herself denying or not acknowledging it. Every night, she stayed up, crying about that night. Even after so many months, it made her terribly sad, scared, and suspicious about what the day that was about to begin would rise up with. She made a decision to tell the officer over the phone about the little that she believed she knew. It made her afraid for her family. She felt it was the right thing, the honourable thing to do.

* * *

The investigation report was not in yet. Chief Grant lumbered around his cabin like a restless bear, hungry for his meal. The body was so battered, they said reports would come only on Monday. Two days he had to wait, it was unnerving, inescapable, disturbing. Most of the people who had come had already made up their minds. The reporters sure had, he noticed.

His office was in a mess, cigarette stubs toppling out of the ashtray, files half opened, papers lying all over his desk—notes lined, double underlined, questions unanswered. It was already evening, pouring heavily outside. The dampness outside manifested inside his cabin, invading his territory, disguised as a throbbing headache.

The sky was trembling purple, as if it was being throttled—lips pouting in a failed attempt to gulp down air, but finding none. A murder, that's what he seemed to see everywhere. It was frustrating, and those eyes, they kept replaying in his head. He saw her reaction, it was like that of a wild animal, frenzied at first, then it turned into something definite. Like a full stop. Even watching her from so far away, he found it uncomfortable. Suddenly she became conscious of him watching her so intently.

She looked at him, and like the changing seasons, her eyes turned innocent, nervous, and guilty.

Officer Scott was stuck in traffic, he had one last house to go to, Mrs. Davis', and he desperately wanted to finish it off today. The weather sure was not going to permit it, it seemed. He was so close to the house, yet if he took this turn, he knew he could get stuck in the traffic for endless hours. He decided to go back to the station since he got a call from Chief Grant, who was waiting for him at the office too. Perhaps, it would be better if he visited Mrs. Davis tomorrow.

By the time he reached the Police Station, it was already late evening. The rain was exhausted too; it was drizzling now. The traffic fizzled out too. In one corner two men were smoking. The lamp post was flickering nearby; a brown stray cat was tearing apart a dead rat. The roads were deserted now mostly. After a heavy shower, it felt like the city had been run through a wash and it was yawning, lazy, and nonplussed. Inside Chief Grant's cabin was quite another feeling. The feeling was dense, evaporated, and pleated together with tension. As soon as Scott entered, he was welcomed with bullets of questions and stale, murky air.

"Did you finish all the houses? Anything significant yet?" Chief Grant badgered.

"No, not yet, one left still—Mrs. Davis. Although I don't think I will find anything of importance there. The other neighbours didn't help really, except Mrs. Smith. I think she may know something important. Even though she didn't say so, I could see it in her behaviour. I have a hunch she will come around eventually," Officer Scott added.

"Mrs. Smith, Baked & Iced, right? Her son has a history of bullying students, could he have something to do with all this? I doubt—though it can't be ruled out. Check it out. Also, Mr. Bob Smith was known to be notorious, not recently, earlier though.

He might know people who could be involved in this sort of barbaric act," Chief Grant said.

"All right, I will check them out at once. Tomorrow I should be done with all of them. What about the forensic report, can't we get it earlier? Any possibility? What do you think about the body?" Officer Scott asked.

"No possibility to get it earlier. Really annoying that things move so much slower here. Can't say anything about the body really. Sometimes I feel positive it is him, other times I feel otherwise," Chief Grant shared, running his fingers to un-crease his temple.

The mind is an amazon in itself, held together by tendrils, weeds, and twigs. For centuries, researchers have tried to break this nutshell and understand, deduce, and standardise it. With every inch forward, we only falter two steps backwards. Encased in suppositions, conflicted emotions, memories. The most dangerous zone of course is the memory, it plunges and dips—distorts notions that we believe true. With time, they enlarge and minimise, exaggerate and fade, overlap and accentuate—until it becomes impossible to really take into account with a high wattage of credibility.

Chapter 16

Banging Doors and Animal Cry

It has been a while since I had last seen Mrs. Davis. With all the high-intensity drama since last week, I thought I deserved this tiny getaway. My mind has been bogged down deeply and nothing at home gives me a sense of peace anymore. Mama has not been keeping well, since that day in the woods. She mostly stays in bed—with her strong medications there is barely anything they allow her to do. Father, on the other hand, has been avoiding talk or any discussion about you. Once again, we all seem to be on this giant wheel—riding on solo seats. We go high up and come down low—experience the void in our tummy, ignore it, and sink our teeth deep into that thick layer of skin under the lower lip to prevent us from screaming. The tenacity of the matter is no more the missing label; it has moved into the death forum now. I don't know if I should call it an advanced stage or a state of retirement.

I have been sneaking out late at night; taking walks more frequently near the woods, just to hear your echo—they say the Redbarrow Woods steal nothing that is not theirs. There is an eeriness in the atmosphere, everything listens, the chirping stops ominously—as I cross length after length. At times, I feel I am being followed or watched. Like I am in a prism and with each turn, a different shape blooms into shape. I simply keep walking, sprinting, stretching myself edge to edge from angle to angle. What changed that night? I know not; what I do know is that I am not afraid any longer.

My walks become longer every night, it's strange that no animal has attacked me yet. Perhaps, they too think I have become one with them—of them? The air feels thin and stagnant at first, but as it approaches dawn, it becomes horizontal and misty out here in the woods. The soft crunch of the dry leaves becomes music to my yearning ears. I smell the sweet-smelling, crisp, and fresh night jasmine as I finally bid adieu to the woods every morning. There is a strange pull of familiarity here. The long grass, creaking branches of the oak trees, pine trees, squirrels chattering, scents carried by the wind, wood smoke. The taste of earthy nuts and berries, wild onions, and mushrooms, tantalises my palate. I love the feel of the coarse tree bark, the hanging moss tickles, and the soft web strands of the unknown spider. All of it becomes like a garb I wear to be able to bear the restlessness of the night.

The gate at Mrs. Davis's house creaks more than usual—it has a lot of undergrowth of weeds and creepers. It almost reminds me of entering the woods—into the wilderness. Maybe I like it here because of that. It wasn't like this always. Earlier she used to keep a very efficient gardener, who kept everything trimmed and groomed. I make a mental note to myself, to check with her why this sudden change of preference. Her quaint porch outside stands beaming at me, the décor is so similar to ours that I frequently mistake it for ours, and feel disoriented at where I am. Yet that's just one of my many quirky slip-ups.

She is outside, dusting her cushions and I notice a water can lying idly near her potted plants. On the small coffee table, she has a letter pad neatly placed with geometric prints on it. It looks new to me. A couple of parker pens and a few fluorescent highlighters are there too. When I approach closer, I hear her humming; her back is turned towards me. There is a sense of calm about her, after a long time. I wonder what has caused this tiny miracle.

We so often miss the tiny miracles in life. A sequence we adorn into our lives and we go about it without appreciating the nitty-gritty of it. Seldom do we realise the difference between leading a life to living one. You, for one always found time to live it. I wonder if expiry comes sooner if we live it so passionately. I don't know really, it's confusing. I walk closer towards the porch. She turns as she hears my footsteps, almost with a jerk. Like she was not expecting anyone.

"Macy! What a surprise! I must have been deep in thought, simply didn't hear you coming. Come in, my dear, how are you doing? How are Polly and Jack?" Mrs. Davis asks welcoming me with an embrace.

"I am well, Mrs. D, how have you been? Been a long time. Mama and Dad are well too. You should come see us some time, they will be happy to see you, you know. You haven't visited us for so long. I thought I must pay you a visit," I say, smiling at her and entering the house.

"Well, I have been busy around the house really, nothing new. I know, I will surely come down some time. Now, you make yourself comfortable, I will be back with some coffee and some freshly baked cakes—marble cake. I hope you like it, Ginny?" Mrs. Davis smiles at me.

"Macy, not Ginny. Sounds lovely, I hope I am not bothering you, Mrs. D?" I sit on the pink couch opposite the bookshelves. The air in the house smells slightly stale, the curtains are open, but the windows are shut. Suddenly I find myself craving some coffee and cake. I explore the bookshelf idly, absent-mindedly. Most of the books I have already read, a few draw my attention, particularly the books on baking. I pull one out and flip through the pages. Indeed, it has some good tips, I notice. I am engrossed in the book when the buzzer rings. Mrs. D calls out to me from the kitchen to answer the door. Putting the book down, I make my way to the door.

By the time I reach the door, the buzzer rings again. Quite impatient, I think to myself, whoever it is. When I open the door, I find the younger police officer (can't seem to place his name somehow), standing there with his back towards me, tapping his sunglasses against his thigh. He turns around at the sound of the unlocking. Our eyes meet and he looks fairly surprised, confused, and unprepared to see me at the receiving end. I understand the confusion—the porch and me of course. Mrs. D yells from inside asking who it is. Before I answer, I hear her come noisily from the kitchen. Hearing her voice, the officer registers he is in the right house and I let him enter.

What happens next is sort of hazy now. A frenetic series of events unfolds. All I remember now is that there was a loud noise from upstairs somewhere. Simultaneously, Mrs. Davis reaches the living room and runs back inside just as she sees the officer and hears the noise. The officer and I also run in to see what that noise is about. We reach halfway through the corridor, when banging doors and an animal cry grip us solid. My heart drives on an accelerated pace, sweat drips down my spine. Instinctively, the officer grabs the gun from its holder and crouches, moving in smooth strides, pushing me behind him with his free hand. All this excitement is too much for me to bear, and I cannot contain it all inside me. Things start to blur, black dots appear, the walls close in on me, and I fall off like a limp, weak leaf on the floor.

When I next gain consciousness, I find myself in familiar surroundings; in my room, tucked under my pink duvet. A tiny streak of amber light peeks at me through my window, and the aircon wheezes at a comfortable temperature. Everything looks and tastes delicious; customised to my tastebuds. I wriggle myself in more cosily and savour it a tad bit longer. Then I try to lift my head from the pillow, when a hammer bangs on my head vindictively and I am compelled to hit it back on the pillow. That is when I recollect all the events that led me here.

The suddenness of it all as it stacks into my memory not so neatly, leaves me jerky, skittish, and dry. I look around and find nobody around me. My annoyance at my helplessness heightens the lurid events that had occurred. Soon I am unable to differentiate the actual from the exaggerated bits. I am thirsty and desperately in need of a drink of water, which is nowhere to be found. I lean, incline myself slightly towards the door, and try to scream for mother, in vain. My voice is cracked, croaks, and is sprinkled like the residual remains from a sprinkler that merely coughs. I can clearly hear loud voices outside my door. Once again, I try to call out, and this time mother does hear me and rushes in.

"Mace, you woke up! We were so worried about you. How are you feeling now?" Mother asked, stroking my hair.

"Mama, I want some water, please. What... happened to me?" was all I managed to concoct.

"I will get some water for you. You just blacked out, perhaps you hadn't eaten anything for a long time. I worry about you," she expressed.

Nothing about that incident she mentioned. Zipped. Before I could ask, she scurried out to get water. She came back with some water, some chicken soup, and some bread rolls. When I tried to broach the subject, she smoothly added in some non-sequiturs and avoided answering the question. The food and soup appeased my curiosity, at least for the time being. The warm liquid poured into my system and immediately oiled it into motion, I felt great and sleepy at the same time. The buttered bread rolls padded me with the much-needed carbs in my body. I enjoyed every bit of my meal, drowning myself into each bite meticulously. Perhaps I even moaned absent-mindedly just a bit too loudly, because mother gave me a disapproving look.

After the meal, I tried to get up. Dad came in to check on me, and along with him, the officer did too. Surprisingly, the genuine concern in his pale grey eyes made my tummy do a whoosh. I chose to ignore it, yet I could feel the rosette hue tinge the tips of my ears almost instantly. He held my eyes for a second too long and then we broke away, diving into the impending questions weighing the air down.

"What happened at Mrs. Davis's house? Where did that noise come from? Did you find out, Officer?" I badgered him before he could initiate.

"Oh! That was nothing. Don't get yourself worked up about it. Mrs. Davis has some old relative visiting her and he stays upstairs away from the sunlight to which he is allergic. It was his lunchtime when we arrived, hence the commotion," the officer explained, although I was not very convinced he believed it himself.

"You need proper rest, Mace, don't get your head wrapped around anything that hampers your health. The doctor said strictly to take rest and I insist on the same," Dad added.

"I must take your leave now, it's been a long day and I appreciate the information you have shared. Will be working on it first thing in the morning. You take rest and get well soon, Macy," the officer said.

I found myself smiling and nodded my head shyly. Dad saw him out, while mother stayed and waited till I got ready for bed. She insisted upon this, afraid I might sink again. They didn't tell me what they spoke to the officer about; I didn't pester them too. I parked that inquiry for the morning. At last, I remembered his name, Officer Scott! Now, I was suddenly in a good mood and I kissed mother goodnight and snuggled back in bed.

Chapter 17

Jerry's Discovery

Another two months passed, and no one knew anything about Jerry Mason still. The uproar had died down, and things started to fall into the usual mundanity. Whatever the police were up to was under wraps. Away from the pestering news reporters. While most assumed the worst, especially the festoon of gossipmongers, sipping their wine and nibbling on their salads, there was also the lot who cared to keep him alive in more ways than one.

Some lit candles and spent evenings remembering him, dedicating verses to him, and praying for his return. It was a quiet affair, soft music, some bonfire, and barbeque; mostly extended family. His college friends wrote with their teachers some letters and cards for his return, filled up a box, and gave it to the Masons.

The festive season was near, already the year-end was near. The Redbarrow was adorning herself slowly, seductively, shyly, bit by bit. She bloomed the most in her winters. Soft specks of snow canopied along the roads, and topped the trees like whipping cream swirls. There are no real ghastly, harsh winters here. It was delicate, gentle, and surreal. The woods had a thicker carpet of snow, yet it was not an intimidating one. It was all still in its nascent stage; not yet settled in completely. The animals had not yet hibernated, they were busy storing food for much later. There was always something odd about winter; it made one hungrier more frequently, even the animals sensed, and experienced that.

Back at Baked & Iced, it was the real business time for them. Bustling with people, there was a constant buzz. Cafes opened and closed—none really could withstand the competition against Baked & Iced. Mrs. Smith was quietly discussing the fresh new menus with her husband. Mr. Smith was a warm, plump man with scanty hair and a laugh that vibrated the entire café. Most identified him as Father Christmas himself. He always smelled of warm loaves of nutty cakes and apple pies. Slightly over sixty, to most of the neighbourhood, he was an adoring husband, a dutiful, loving father, and a responsible and inspiring neighbour.

Although it was an important discussion, Mrs. Smith's mind was elsewhere today. She had made some plans herself, without consulting her husband or children. Which was a first. Normally she depended on their opinions and suggestions very heavily. Being slightly on the edge, she found it difficult to concentrate. Time tiptoed out of those menus like crawling cursive letters, a fading second nudging the next one. Mr. Smith was too occupied and hassled with the planning, so didn't notice her restlessness. At last, the discussion came to an end. By the end of it though, Mr. Smith found it strange how she agreed to everything he said; contradicting nothing, which was out of the ordinary. Yet he was not the type to Sherlock his way around his wife whom he deeply loved and trusted. Mrs. Smith slipped out of the café and hailed a cab.

* * *

The air was acrid, prosaic, and sticky in the room. The only source of light was starved, suffocated through the tiny window—merely an eye could fit through it. It was midday, and the noise outside was deafening. Jerry Mason sat on the edge of his bed with his fingers shoved intrusively inside his ears. The lower half of his body shook unrhythmically, head bent down. His hair had grown long, and his body was lean, and toned with the constant exercise he indulged in. In that small attic, there were no mirrors. If he could see himself in a mirror, it would take him a couple of minutes to recognise himself. Alone, he spent most of his time reading, writing, and exercising.

The endless uncertainty was like a virus spreading rapidly and weakening his willpower. His thoughts kept running back to that day when he had heard voices downstairs. The temptation was too strong not to create chaos, and draw attention. That was when he decided to crash the study table. For a few seconds, he could hear multiple pairs of footsteps coming his way, yet in the end, only a pair sounded close enough and the chaos died down. He believed it was an opportunity that simply slipped away. The resolve became stronger that day, that perhaps he could escape from here one day.

Over the months, his hallucinations had started increasing. Frequently at night, he could hear Mrs. Davis's voice whispering into his ear. He would wake up sweating and chug down water thirstily—splashing water on his face. It made him wistful. He thought about the times he had spent with her and found himself missing that dear old lady. Some nights he fell asleep, talking to his little Mace. A blubbering mess he became, telling her how much he hated it here, the disorientation he experienced, and how he hated all those times they wasted squabbling with each other. Until he found no more strength, and finally fell asleep. He slept with a light on, no more did he trust the darkness. Something changed that night and he was estranged from the darkness completely. Like he could never trust it again.

He missed the Redbarrow Woods desperately. Before the crack of dawn, he would lie awake—press his eyes shut, and try to imagine running his palm against the reddish-brown trunk of the oak tree. Imagine himself getting lost in that labyrinth—gasping for breath—never stopping. These episodes became more visually real as time looped and every time the return from there diminished. A sense of freedom he could taste, hungrily he gorged on it until it faded and what remained was a piercing headache.

One night, he experienced an odd event. Like every night, his food came in, and then after an hour, he slipped it under the door. There was something he noticed that was pronounced. He didn't hear the door being bolted from the outside. Maybe, they forgot it in a hurry? Or perhaps, it was a test for him, what if he was simply imagining it? Did they want to see if he would escape and then capture him and torture him more? These questions strobed at the back of his mind.

He paced around the tiny room like a lion restless to pounce. He waited for another two hours, it was beyond midnight now. He twisted the door knob, pressing it mutely. He walked out of the door. Nothing. No one was there to attack him. Fingers trembling, heart jumping out of his mouth—like a fox he walked down the stairs and then froze.

* * *

The cab driver was the talkative kind, he kept on bantering about how he wanted to become a chef, and here he was driving a car. In normal circumstances, Mrs. Smith would have loved to hear all about his miseries and his passion for cooking. She might even have given him a chance at her café. Like she had to many newcomers… She liked helping people, that was simply her innate quality. Today, however, was not really that day. Her posture was alert, defensive, and jittery. She took turns between rearranging her purse and shifting on her seat. She simply couldn't get the right position.

The drive into the woods was longer than she expected. She didn't see anybody at the bridge, which she found strange. She had clearly mentioned to Officer Scott to meet her there at 3 p.m. sharp. She was beginning to think this was a terrible idea and was on the verge of telling the driver to turn back when she heard a sharp knock on her window. Officer Scott's face smiling at her made her almost jump out of the car.

"Good afternoon, Mrs. Smith, how are you doing? Hope I didn't scare you?" Officer Scott said.

"Good afternoon, Officer, I am quite all right. Let's get this done with, shall we?" Mrs. Smith whispered, exasperated. From inside her purse, she took the pink sticky note and handed it over to him. Officer Scott opened it and read it.

"What is this? I don't understand this phrase. Even the Masons told me about it. I am unable to reach anywhere with it. Where did you get it? What link does this have with Jerry Mason?"

"The night that Jerry Mason disappeared, he had come down to the café like he usually did. That evening he was not himself; something was on his mind. He ordered his apple crumble and coffee and sat aloof. Which was unlike him. He was usually chatty and warm. He was mumbling something to himself, like he was trying to memorise it. After he left, one of my boys found this pink sticky note with this writing on it. I kept it, thinking it must be something important. Later that night we heard the scream and he disappeared. I don't know if this has any importance, yet I felt it was my duty to give it to you, just in case. I did tell Polly about this, yet just not in so many words. I only mean to help."

Officer Scott nodded his head and watched her like a hawk. He slipped the note into his wallet and thanked her for her support. He arranged for a cab for her and told her he would be in touch. In the cab, Mrs. Smith felt lighter, as if a load had been lifted from her. She had done her bit of moral duty; it made her feel good.

Officer Scott reported back to the station to update the Chief. Chief Grant looked up from his file as he entered. Scott looked at his Chief. He had deep dark circles under his eyes, his hair was a mess, overgrown too. A shiver ran down his spine.

He wondered if he looked pretty much as ghastly as his chief. Something on the table arrested his attention. It was the file of the investigation on the dead body found.

"Sir, that picture looks familiar, is it…? Did you get the detailed analysis of the body?"

"Scott, you are right, that picture is unnerving. It looks like Jerry Mason. Before I get to it, I need you to do a couple of things for me, first thing tomorrow morning. What did Mrs. Smith say, anything significant to help on the case?

"Sir, you always do this. At least tell me about this report. Mrs. Smith gave me this note." He pulled it out of his wallet and gave it to Grant. Grant stared at it and then gave it back to him. He ran his fingers through his hair and banged the table.

"Again, this phrase. What is going on? I simply don't understand, seriously. That's it, Scott, get to the bottom of this and come back to me. Did you hear me? I don't care if you have to go to the moon. Just get it done," he said and stormed out of the office, leaving Scott staring at that picture on the desk. Scott went back to his desk, to pan out the next day. He narrowed down the list to the people who might have heard this phrase and where. By the time he finished, it was late at night. He noticed the light was still on in Grant's office. He admired the diligence and dedication that his Chief put in even after reaching such a high position. It drove him to work harder, he realised, to be working under such a legend, and it was an inspiration, he truly believed.

Somewhere the night had ascended, yet somewhere it was sinking between the shadows of apprehensions. The night owl hooted nonchalantly while a film of dust carried whispers of forbidden deeds. A mother yearned for her estranged son, clinging to his leftover memories. Behind the thick brown curtain, an old man with a pipe in his hand peeped, wondering what his wife was up to. The lonely girl walked with her head down, rubbing her arms as she shivered under her thin sweatshirt. Not very far away, a muffled cry died under two pillows. Stains of guilt stubbornly refused to wear out; cloaking the street with a thick stench of unholy deeds.

Nothing evades the night; it only leaves it more pronounced.

Chapter 18

Good News

I woke up cold in the middle of the night, my dreams also feeling like a jigsaw puzzle—flashes of one event, then another. I could have sworn someone was projecting slides to tempt me—tempt me into what I honestly didn't want to know. My bedside lamp was flickering, and the aircon was coughing like an old man. I am a fairly sound sleeper, but of late the trend had shot up in a different tangent altogether. There were chunks of voids in my memory lately—like in the fourth grade I wanted an elaborate kitchenette for my birthday and you wanted a shiny red mountaineer bicycle for yours. One summer we were playing hide and seek in the woods. I was hiding and you were supposed to find me. I remember being yelled at. Do you remember the time I was chosen for elocution on the School founders' day? I was so excited; it was my first solo performance. Blank. Blank. Blank.

I can never forget those winter vacations, when all four of us drove up the hills to camp—there were a bonfire, barbeque, and horror stories, and we did some trekking too. The best part was the water sports we jumped into. I met with a bad fall while rafting. Recently I was flipping through photographs and found our birthday party pics. That huge bouncy castle at your ninth birthday party. You were so obsessed with superheroes; you had a different one as your cake every year. The best thing about your birthday parties was the endings when you would recite a long poem you had written yourself. I can still hear the applause—it sounded like a thrust of rainfall falling on the moaning earth, the ravings about how good you were getting every year. Most importantly, mother and father were so very proud of you, we all were. Everyone was so much in awe of you.

Even when I was a little girl, you always looked out for me. When I first started walking, you would stand around me ready to catch me when I fell. Always the doting brother you have been. I remember the time I fell sick; you would stay awake all night until the fever receded. Do you remember the time I got bullied for the first time in college? You came to my class the next day to give those chaps a piece of your mind. All the students were either in love with you or were petrified of your guts. My friends were jealous of me; they wished their brothers were as protective, caring, and loving. I never did understand that.

Mother worried about you all the time; you were her precious always. If you came late from school, when a teacher picked on you (a rarity though), she made at least one of your favourite dishes every single day—although she would always deny any purposeful intention of doing the same. Her slice of apple strudel, she always nibbled on it, waiting for you to finish yours so she could offer it to you, feed you hers as well, even though it is her favourite too. The list was unending, to the point that it felt exhausting to me. Dad spent way too much time planning your future, you were his golden prince. He was not overtly expressive, yet his way of expressing it, was like thunder rumblings you hear—I could always feel it right under my ribcage, the explosion of warmth. Perhaps, I noticed all these things and felt them so strongly because I was hungry.

The bed was making me feel caged with all these thoughts pinning me down. I felt trapped in this opinion of mine. All of a sudden, the night felt old to me—like it had suddenly become too frail to hold onto me. The thing is, it had witnessed my longing, my tears, and my anger for too long. I opened the curtains to scan the sky—to inquire when it would break open again. Starless it was tonight, a quaking, quivering stillness arrested me. Yet it was not silent, it was heavy—I could feel the weight of unanswered pleas, yellow stains of dried-up tears, the stinging red shade of bitter confessions.

I was so engaged in my thoughts; I almost missed the sounds coming from inside the house. I switched on the lights and walked into the living room, and found Mama drinking water—sitting with slumped shoulders, and dazed eyes, sighing heavily. She was tense, we all were. All for the same reason, but with different motives, oddly. Oodles of sorrow webbed her face, which was older, forlorn with grief. She didn't like being discovered in this state, I know that for a fact. So, I watched her for a few more seconds and slid back into my room. Sometimes no conversations make the best confessions, you had said that once. Now, I understand it.

Tomorrow is a big day. The officers had called in the evening. It's the big reveal. That is what has been on all our minds. I guess Dad too called in absent from his office. We didn't talk much about it; you know how we all zone out with worry. Sometimes, I wish we were more expressive, like other families. Then, we would be less dysfunctional as a family you know. Yet wishes blow into big bubbles into the sky. Poof! I have realised one thing; you were the strongest link that wound us all together, and I know you were not even aware of that fact.

The temperature had dipped rapidly; it was scalding cold. Exhaustion got to me from brain down. Putting aside me and my thoughts, I tucked myself under the covers. I trembled under the quilt. Isn't it odd that the quilts are always so cold without human contact? They are meant to keep us warm, only they can't do much without us. Deeds of life are so much alike—cold, undone, strange thoughts. Until we, humans, decide to put them into action, for good or evil, and they become ours to own. Pressing my toes together, wriggling myself down under it, I tried to induce warmth. It worked, lulling me back into a deep siesta.

The day was already well advanced when I woke up. I could hear a lot of chaos from outside. It took a few seconds to register, the events that were lined up for the day. Jumping out of bed, I almost tripped and fell. The buttery light filtered into the room. My room smelled faintly caramelised; an alluring sweetness tinged it. Already I could sense the mood in the house—frigid to the touch—sensitive and prone to eruption.

Fumbling through my closet, I found a faded pair of olive-green coloured chinos pants and a crumpled coral shirt. I didn't really bother much with my appearance with the anxiety roiling inside me. Brushing my hair into a messy knot, I stole one last glance at the mirror. They might have already arrived or were about to reach. My mind was in a mad race as to what to expect from this meeting. When I finally stepped out, it felt like I was late for assembly at school. Sheepishly, I shrugged my shoulders and sank into the sofa near mother. All four of them were sitting at the dining table and discussing with interrupted jagged silences. The electricity in the room told me they must have just arrived; revelations were yet to take place. I caught Officer Scott's eye; I believe we shared a moment of greetings and his eyes twinkled in a nod. Not wanting to get distracted, I looked away a little too quickly, reluctantly.

"The reason we are here today, is to reveal some good news and some bad news. Now, which one should we start with?" asked Chief Grant.

"Why don't you start with the good news, we have had enough of the bad ones for almost a year now," Father piped in. I couldn't agree more.

"Right you are, Mr. Mason, as you please. The good news is that, the body we found was not Jerry Mason's. We will be making an official statement on the same and our search is very much on."

Everyone did seem relieved to hear the good news. Certainty was what we all needed at this point in time. That faint ray of hope was really all that we could cling to at this point. We waited now, for the bad news.

"The bad news, is that we still haven't found any trace on that phrase you shared with us. You can rest assured we will crack it down

eventually," Chief Grant said. He sort of reminded me of our PE teacher, slightly too earnest and hassled all the time.

"But Chief, did you find out whose body it is?" I asked, making everyone stare at me.

"Good question. That is still not confirmed. We are trying to find out. That was a recent death, it has been discovered a little after a fortnight of the occurrence. It will take a while, we are on it. In the immediate neighbourhood, no one is missing—so we need to look at the outskirts. At the max it will be a matter of two weeks," Chief Grant said.

"This is so strange, poor kid, his parents must be distraught with him gone. I can understand their state completely," Mother whimpered in sadness.

"Chief, it has already been eight months; we have not heard from him. Is there still hope left, I mean, all we want to know desperately is that can we hope that he is alive—out there somewhere. Honestly, as the months are strangulating on, I have started losing hope completely now. Perhaps, only a few strands of hope are left, those too fading soon enough," Dad confessed morosely.

I was staring at the plate of sausages, congealed scrambled eggs, and toast browned a tad bit too much. My stomach growled so loudly, for a second, I could feel all their eyes on me. Mother whispered into my ears and told me to clear these plates and go into the kitchen and eat. I was so grateful to her for that brilliant piece of advice, I could almost cry. Sliding off my chair as mutely as I could, I stretched out my hands across the table to pick up the plates. Inside the kitchen, I felt light-headed as I sank my teeth into the toast that had been heaped with scrambled eggs. The goodness of food is unforgiving, truly—the sheer bliss as it lines the tummy cannot be described any better than that guttural groan that involuntarily escapes wickedly.

Outside in the dining room, they were still talking solemnly. I couldn't hear clearly, only random words I picked up, and now I was not so interested. I looked outside and thought about the revelations they had made today. The stillness of the light created a facade through the window. As if curtains had been drawn, it matched the calmness I was wearing. The cold marble table top felt good under my palm. I smiled—a streak of relief flooded me. Ever since the cops had informed us about that body and then that they would be coming today, I had been nervous. Although, I found it different from the kind mother and father were feeling. Mine was stranger. Now too, their relief was of a separate genre from my mine. Gulping down hot coffee, the smell of caffeine mixed with bits of my relief let out a small smirk—a triumphant one. After a long time, it felt good. To strip away that annoying mask I have to wear in front of everyone. I did allow myself to giggle a bit uninhibitedly and then I swallowed the release of the emotions, afraid someone might see me. I could feel a pair of eyes on my back and I quickly put on the act.

Chapter 19

The Postman

Ms. Mary Murphy liked to walk on the beach every evening. The feel of wet sand squashed between her toes was liberating for her. Every bone and fibre in her body felt empowered. The waves drooled and licked her wet. It tickled—the ripples smelled of the cold sun and seaweed and were salty. Gradually, she would go further into the sea, and the foam would welcome her animatedly chattering away. It made her smile. She always felt so much at home here. Yet today her conscience was not at peace. For a while, she had been thinking about it. It had been more than a month since Officer Scott had visited her. Something was bothering her about that day. As if she couldn't remember something important that day. With age, it had started becoming more frequent. Usually, she just let it pass; with the increasing number of things she forgot, she just let go. This felt crucial, to find that boy. Her dear boy.

The sea always calmed her nerves. Calm nerves made her feel and think better. Sequence-wise she sketched out the last few days before the disappearance. There was more colour in his face, he looked like he was working with his hands more. It was doing wonders to his toned body. Was it the old-age home he was helping at or somewhere else she couldn't put a finger on? That last day, he was in a hurry, he had to go and help someone—sort out things perhaps. Then she remembered. That's it. She couldn't wait to tell Officer Scott.

* * *

"Mama!" screamed Jerry. Polly Mason, with arms stretched out, tried to pull Jerry from the red flames that licked him hungrily right in the middle of their living room. Her son was trembling, frightened, burning right in front of her eyes. With every lash against his skin, the flame grew richer, larger. She couldn't reach him. Immobile, as if her feet were planted in the ground, her voice was lodged deep inside her throat, and no sound came out. She was distraught with desperation, nothing she did was aiding her in rescuing her son. Suddenly his eyes turned glassy, frozen as if realisation, recognition struck him and he stopped screaming. An ominously sad smile played on his face, he closed his eyes and inhaled the flames. Polly's face contorted in confusion, her mouth opened wider, and tears streamed down faster.

Her helplessness heightened—clutching the bedsheet she writhed from side to side. When she woke up, Jack was by her side stroking her into an embrace while she sobbed uninhibitedly. Her thoughts kept going back to that meeting with the cops, their big revelation—that it was not the body of Jerry Mason. The mere 'if' was like a streak of current shooting into her and she couldn't get it out of her system. Biting her lower lip, she stopped the shudders that were subsiding slowly.

* * *

I wish the night would cradle me, like it does the sky. I can see that yellow light flickering from the window; I think someone is cooking. The thought makes me want to cry, yet I don't. I remember the warmth of her skin, when I would surprise hug her from behind. She used to be so engrossed in her cooking, that she never did notice me creeping up behind her. The smell of caramelised beans, carrots, and cauliflowers lying limp next to the glistening brown skin of the chicken. There is no sound from downstairs tonight. His stomach groaned, and growled indignantly, dinner was late tonight. *Did they forget to give me dinner*? Jerry Mason whispered to himself.

A strong smell of varnish wafted into his room. The window had a fresh coat of mist on it outside. He ran his hands against the window pane. Nothing happened. A yawn intervened into his thoughts. Sleep crept up on him seductively. *Tomorrow will be a promising day*, he whispered to himself, every night.

* * *

The night was not done yet. Chief Grant and Officer Scott were still at the station, racking their heads over the identity of the dead body. Most of the technical work was done by the forensic team. They were on the last leg, scanning the list of missing people in Redbarrow. None of them were fitting the description of the deceased yet. Exhaustion sapped them bitterly and they barely had a head to assist them now. It was two-thirty at night when Chief said it was time to give it a rest and put some food in their tummies. Cold slices of pizza with coke they gulped down hungrily.

"Chief, do you think we are looking at the wrong places, maybe? Is it possible we should be looking at some other list? I am not sure, just a gut feeling," Scott said with his mouth full of cheese and barbequed chicken.

"Scott, don't talk in riddles. I don't have the energy for that. Tell me clearly what you mean," Chief said, chugging coke down.

"I am really thinking aloud here, don't know the specifics. What if the person was not missing, his body was disposed of, or just left to rot after his death?"

"Let's go through what we know as of now. The body was in his late twenties or early thirties; he was fit—more than a normal citizen's standard. Cause of death, several injuries, about eight months old. Exactly the same time as Jerry Mason went missing."

"Someone knows something. Yet they're not ready to tell us. There was a postman who has recently retired, he could know something. He doesn't work anymore. I can check with him tomorrow morning. What do you think, Chief?"

"No harm in trying, touch base with him tomorrow. I think we should call it a night. Get some rest, Scott. I am leaving too."

"Sure Chief, you have a good night."

* * *

Drawing the curtains, Officer Scott watched the auburn dawn peel away the dark shavings of dusk. The shavings fell over clumsily as riddles in his head. He could barely sleep at night. Disturbing images of the lonesome, unidentified dead body loomed everywhere. Sipping his extra-strong Espresso, he thought about the two boys. So much similarity between the two, he thought to himself. One lost in death, the other in life, both young boys—adjourned promising futures. Mothers pining for their sons, families trying to fill this void—only it sharpened as grief honed it mercilessly. Perhaps, one was a friend of the other, or they had crossed paths in this life, or maybe brushed shoulders against each other in death?

The thing with an unsolved mystery was that it left him gasping for peace. Yet until it was solved, he never found it. Just as he was deep in thought, his phone beeped loudly.

"Officer Scott, this is Ms. Murphy, you remember? I wanted to meet with you today. I remembered something that might be important related to Jerry Mason's disappearance."

"Sure, Ms. Murphy, tell me where and when, I will be there."

"Can you come home in the evening around four?"

"I will be there."

Officer Scott couldn't contain his excitement. Any progress in the case added to solving the mystery. He gobbled up some toast with jam and left home in search of the postman. The postman lived in a small apartment near the post office. Due to his long tenure with the post office, it was fairly easy to locate him. When he rang the bell, the postman's wife answered the door. She looked haggard—dark circles under her eyes, strands of hair flying into her face, her body speaking of malnutrition. She trembled and was perturbed to see Officer Scott.

"I am looking for the postman who recently retired, Mr. Timothy Parker. Is he home? This is important, it would be of great help if he could share some information."

"Uh oh, yes, he is home. Please come inside. I am sorry, the house is in a mess, we were not expecting anyone. My husband is not keeping well these days. Doctor has advised him bed rest and to keep him calm. Most days, he doesn't talk at all. Sometimes he forgets who I am. Honestly, I don't know how much help he will be."

"I am so sorry to hear that. I am desperate here, if I can at least try once. This should not take time; I will be out here before you know."

Mrs. Susan Parker nodded unsmilingly and took him into the bedroom. There was a damp, musty stench in the room. As if clothes had been drying in an enclosed area. A crooked lamp was placed near the bed; the light flickered. The windows were closed, and there was one rectangular bookshelf, one desk, and a chair. There was a thick film of dust on all the furniture. In one corner, a frail man lay on the bed, staring at the ceiling fan above him. His bald head was the only shiny thing in the room. At the shuffling footsteps, he stirred his head. He looked at them, with a slightly terrified look, not making eye contact—he looked beyond them.

Mrs. Parker pulled out the chair and offered it to Scott. Scott was disheartened by the sight that welcomed him. His heart sank, and he sighed as he sat down. Was this going to be a futile visit, he wondered.

"Mr. Parker, I am Officer Scott, I have heard so much about you. Everyone you have served and delivered mail to—they all have wonderful things to say about you—at the office and the neighbours. It is a pleasure to meet you in person."

No response, no eye contact.

"Well today, I am here for some information. We have recently found a dead body. Not sure if you have heard about it. We have not identified the deceased as yet. So far, we know that he was a young lad, late twenties or early thirties, very fit in health, and he died about eight months back. Around the same time Jerry Mason, son of Jack Mason went missing. I am not sure the stories are linked—the timing just seems odd. Anything you remember—being regular in that neighbourhood, something we might have missed. It would be of great help."

Nothing. He continued to stare at the fan. Scott looked at Mrs. Parker. She gave him the 'I told you so look' and shrugged nonchalantly. He looked at the postman and gave it one last try while Mrs. Parker went into the kitchen and put on the kettle reluctantly.

"Anyone, mother or father you remember who had a son, perhaps he was far away? They wrote letters to him? Some kid in a boarding school or working abroad. Only came to see his family for a short while? If there is anything at all you remember that you can think of during that time. Please, I would be so grateful," Officer Scott bent forward and whispered softly before getting up.

Before leaving, he stopped and turned towards Mr. Parker once again and mentioned, "Did you know Jerry Mason? He was probably very little when you were around. It has already been eight months now. You knew everyone in the neighbourhood so well, even a tiny thing that you may think is irrelevant may save a boy's life."

As Officer Scott was about to walk out of the door, he heard a sound from behind. Mrs. Parker was bending over Mr. Parker as he shook his hand vigorously in a writing motion. She hurried to get a pen and paper. Scott walked back towards him and patiently waited. After scribbling something on the piece of paper, he handed it to Scott, with a small smile of reassurance. When he opened and read the paper, Scott had a stunned look on his face. Disbelief danced in his eyes as he read it again and again.

He stretched out his hands and took Mr. Parker's in his hands. Giving it a firm press of gratitude, he turned around and said to Mrs. Parker, "Thank you so much for your cooperation. If there is anything at all I can do, please don't hesitate to reach out. Here is my card."

"I hope you find that boy, Officer. My husband hasn't shown interest in anything in the longest time. This looks like a ray of progress I can hold onto," Mrs. Parker said with tears in her eyes.

Book III

Chapter 20

Denial Mechanism

The Woods and I have nothing in common, except, we have everything in common. The echoes of its silence reverberate inside me. I live in this silence, my eyes shutterbug life around me, mutely. I find solace as people lean on me—just like those thickly rooted oak trees do. When they have an ache they cannot share easily, somewhere deep, I like to make it easy for them to unburden it into words. The moss—sometimes I feel like the stark green coloured moss, growing in damp habitats, flowerless, lacking true roots, is me. My loneliness, regrets, inhibitions all find home here—in the deep crevices of the forest. From the sun-kissed petrichor smell to the musty, grainy fragrance of the fungi, all enliven my senses. Alert like an animal ready to attack his prey, that's how my thoughts phrase and engage into action here. Every time I am here in the woods, I feel like I have planted a piece of myself here. One day I will collect all those pieces and make home here, right amidst this wilderness, I decide.

You remember the gaps in my memory I told you about? I have started realising why I have those now. It's a denial mechanism that my brain has built inside me. Come to think of it, it feels like I always knew. The brain does function in mysterious ways, none can really tell, you know. So, in these woods, as I frequented my visits, things started clearing in my head. The clutter, that has been living inside me like a parasite. At first, it felt so familiarly unfamiliar, like

I was entering a stranger's body. Then, it started making sense, each incident clicked like a perfect picture.

It was as if a thick fog had been stripped, sucked, wiped away. The first rains—yes that's how it felt when things started making sense. I could taste the freshness tingle on my tongue, beady, exotic. With my mouth open wide, I gulped this nectar of revelation. Each incident cracked open for me, as if blooming like a flower—soaking in the goodness of the rains. The elaborate kitchenette I wanted in the fourth grade, which I truly wanted—I never got it, instead, I was given a pink teddy bear. Why? Because I was too little to be taken seriously. That summer when I was hiding and you couldn't find me—I was yelled at because I was too little to hide, and could have got lost. I was so excited about my elocution, yet when I got up on stage, in spite of looking everywhere in the audience, I found no one. Perhaps, I was too little for them to take out time for me?

The rest, as they say, was history. That didn't go down too well for me. Be it my birthday parties, which were never as grand as yours, or so many other hurtful things. These are just a few instances, there are plenty of them, and honestly, I don't want to get into each one of them—when I felt like I didn't belong in the same space as you. Initially, I was unfettered by all this, but then things piled up. Before I knew, it became ugly, it stared back at me when I looked in the mirror. It manifested all around me, like the way she looked at you was always different from the way she looked at me. I found myself caving in, walls, ceiling, the ground, cracking and sucking me in. I felt suffocated, small, and unwanted all of a sudden.

I still remember the incident that triggered it: it was a day that didn't see the sun, the sky was a shade of cobalt bluish grey. Clear cloudless expanse, something very unsettling about that day from the moment it cracked into existence, come to think of it. I was in the kitchen early in the morning—humming to myself, kneading dough for a fresh batch of buns for dinner. Potatoes were chattering loudly in the pot of hot water getting dressed for the creamy mashed potatoes. The chicken I marinated in some Indian spices.

I wanted to try a different grilled chicken I had read about in a new book, one with an Indian touch. The bright red chilli powder, earthy turmeric powder, a spoonful of pungent tandoori masala, a dollop of ginger garlic paste—all of this mixed in some hung curd, salt, and lemon juice. It looked so rich, bright, coming alive—the explosion of flavours was exotic. When I marinated the chicken in it, it started singing in joy, so pretty it looked all dressed up. Over it, I drizzled some mustard oil, and immediately the gashes soaked up the spices. I couldn't wait for it to caramelise in its juices in the oven.

As you can guess, my mood was going places with the food around me cultivating goodness inside. All of you were still in bed asleep—it was one of those lazy winter holidays. I wanted it to be a pleasant surprise. Do you remember that day? The rest of the day was more or less uneventful. We had a lazy breakfast, played scrabble—giggled as we caught Dad cheating. Early evening, I heated the oven and was preparing to put the chicken inside. Mama and Dad were lounging in the living room watching the news and you were in your room. You were going out to a movie with your friends.

I hurried with the dinner so you could have it before you left. The mashed potatoes were almost done, the grilled broccoli, carrots, and peas were sizzling away. The smell in the air was electric. I still remember the flavours flirting gloriously. Finally, I was putting the chicken in the oven. I placed the tray in the oven, but it moved and was about to fall. In that moment, I touched the flaming hot tray with my bare fingers accidentally. The sensation was electric. It ran up and down my spine. I left it immediately and screamed like an animal. Mama came running and was about to put an ice pack on my hand when you yelled for her—something about not finding your favourite blue shirt.

She left the icepack on the marble slab next to me and went to attend to you. That moment something changed in me for you—our relationship chipped. I found myself forgetting about the pain and a strong urge usurped my attention. I wanted to take your head and shove it in the oven. For what it's worth, I myself was surprised by the intensity of this emotion.

Have you ever hated something so much that you mistook that intensity for love, not once but repetitively? Where the lines blur, smudge, smear until it gets so messy that you simply cannot erase either of them? You feel entangled in these chains so bad, that they leave lacerations not only externally but also internally. This feeling grows with time, sort of greasy over the years. Peculiarly, it never grows familiar, it's always there—this stranger and you are conscious of it all the time. Does this sound sane to you? I don't know why, I simply think you are the only one who can understand what I am trying to explain. You sort of always had this serenity about stacking the pieces of puzzles, problems, emotions chronologically—always in order, that was you, Jerry.

If I say I hate you, I would be lying, but if I say I love you, I would be in denial. Circumstances are silly, now with you gone for so long I cannot run away from the facts sneering back at me. I told you something chipped that day. It felt as if something was grating our relationship, the solidarity diminished gradually—somewhere underneath, it became a powdery substance that free-flowed. Even if I tried, it didn't mould back together—I held a fistful of it, but it sieved through the gaps of my fingers. Then one day, I stopped trying to put it all together. That was the time when I couldn't understand why my friends were so jealous of me for having a brother like you. It was unfathomable at that point.

You on the other hand, always unaware, continued to be the caring, loving, and protective brother. That was the confusing part. I couldn't be "the mean me" to you. Simply couldn't take it all out on you.

The genuineness of your love was so pronounced. Every time I tried, something broke in me, it just felt wrong. Those days were terrible, very difficult to put on the farce in front of all of you. Now, thinking back, I wish I had shared some of this with you. Perhaps, you could have wiped away this dreariness I was getting sucked into? Or maybe not.

What it was really doing was, it was eating me from inside. I needed to find a solution, before I lost myself completely. My desperation was getting hungrier; I was failing to feed it contentment. I walked around like a vagrant searching for a home—a solution. Every night I would sit down at my study table, and plan and plot. Only nothing seemed ideal. Of course, I was primarily afraid. I didn't want to hurt you or harm you, at least most of the time. A few times, I wanted to do some terrible things, even thinking about them makes my skin scorch.

Then, one day I found a way. The perfect way to put an end to my misery. It was not a very easy plan. Yet it was just what I needed. By mere accident, I came across this idea. I was not even looking there. You know how they say, when you are most oblivious, things percolate in front of you most blindingly. I guess I pretty much witnessed that.

* * *

For a change, it was very quiet at the Baked & Iced when Officer Scott walked in. Christmas was just around the corner. Everything was lit up so brightly, the mood warmly festive—reds, greens, and whites predominantly danced from every sphere. It was barely five in the morning; the café was just opening up. When he opened the doors, the bells tingled from different corners, freshly toasted cinnamon with melted butter wafted around deliciously. Officer Scott went across the display counter and ordered his regulars: Black coffee, two slices of multigrain toast with *bocconcini*, and tomato slices.

Of late his meals had been irregular, there were dark, hollow bags under his eyes. Sleepless nights and a lot of stress over the ongoing case had taken a toll on his usually healthy habits. Mr. Smith greeted him at the counter. They shared the usual banter about the weather and the festive season. Scott chose a table at the end of the café—slightly aloof, where they could discuss without being heard. He was early as usual, he liked to be ahead of time—it sort of gave him time to prepare himself for the unexpected.

He had to cancel the meeting last evening with Ms. Murphy, so they had rescheduled it for the morning. Ms. Murphy was also an early riser, so they agreed at such an early hour. He was smiling to himself as he thought about his meeting with Mr. Parker. He had given him a solid lead into the dead body's identity. It made him happy that his foresight had resulted in such progress. He wondered staring at his watch, what was in store in this meeting. Looking at his watch, he found himself reminiscing about another time—sitting in the park with her brown wavy locks on his lap, her chatter overlapping with her giggles. Every year, at this time of the year, his wounds would break open and bleed excruciatingly until he became completely numb. Even though he promised himself he would not suffer the next year, his attempts became fragmented and futile. Everyone had a story they didn't want to share; not ready to share rather. This one was Scott's.

Just as he was sipping his coffee, he saw Ms. Murphy entering the café. She seemed even more petite in her long burgundy overcoat. She waved her hand and smiled as she caught his eye. Her gait was slow—given her age and the cruel weather. He found himself feeling sorry for her and immensely grateful too for making the effort in helping with the case. He stood up to assist her to sit down. She ordered a couple of beetroot and cucumber sandwiches and a cappuccino.

She looked around at the other tables, to see if there was anyone close enough to hear her. Not that she was scared of anyone, she just wanted to ensure her Jerry didn't have any more problems than he already had; what if they tortured him more, even the thought made her cringe.

"Thank you for calling me, Ms. Murphy. I am sorry I couldn't meet you yesterday. It's just that something very urgent had come up," Scott explained.

"That's alright, I can completely understand; cops always have to be prepared for the unexpected. The thing is, after you left that day, something was nagging me at the back of my mind. I couldn't place it at that point. So, I thought and thought really hard, and then finally it came to me. I am not sure if it will be of much use. But still, I thought to myself, what if it does help, you know? I was influenced by what you had told me earlier—any information could be helpful," Ms. Murphy confessed.

"Let me stop beating around the bush and get to the point. You remember, I had told you the last time that just before his disappearance, he was very occupied with someone; helping at their house. Usually, he never mentioned the details and I never did probe further. Now I wish I had, though. That last day I heard him on the phone telling someone, he was going to have to cancel their plan as he had urgent work at house number 46," Ms. Murphy whispered even though there was no one within earshot.

Officer Scott listened intently with big eyes not blinking once. Then he nodded his head and scribbled the details on his pad. This could be a big lead; he felt happy and couldn't wait to investigate more into this. They finished their breakfast and he stood up to leave and thanked Ms. Murphy once again, telling her to keep him posted in case she remembered anything else. She smiled and assured him she would.

Outside the café, he pulled out his phone to call the Chief. In his excitement, he couldn't stop grinning like a teenager. Back at the Police Station, Grant listened to Scott over the phone. He told Scott not to return to the station, but instead to go and check the house immediately. The faster they progressed, the closer they would be to cracking the case, he said. Scott reaffirmed this and left the café.

The whirring wind outside house number 46 crackled a little bit. There was an anticipation humming, the ground was damp, and the flowers withered. Creepers and vines overlapped onto the porch. The smell of sweet jasmine mixed with the musty smell inside the house. As if no one lived there—mere memories, guilt, and conspiracies.

Chapter 21

Jerry's Desperation

The jerk of familiarity was like a slap ringing into his ears. At the back of his mind, he had guessed this was possible—his heart was not ready to believe it. A small tiny cry of why imploded inside him. Irrelevant to what the mind said, his heart felt too heavy to carry this any longer. Like a million needles pierced him, he felt paralysed. He could escape right this moment, he knew in his gut. Those myriads of questions gutted him dysfunctional. Everything seemed foggy in his head. As if he had been admonished. He had no idea what he had done, he bent his head down, turned back, and took long strides back up to the attic. Once he reached the attic, he closed the door softly and went to sit down on the bed that had become familiar to him now.

From behind the thick green curtain of the master bedroom, someone was watching without blinking, clutching the curtain in one hand and a knife in the other hand. Ready to attack if he attempted to escape. The tension was electric. She didn't even realise she was holding her breath until Jerry Mason turned back up the stairs. And then she sighed heavily. A smug look stared back at her from the mirror on the other side when she turned back to return to bed. It was a test—she wasn't sure at all what he would do. A risk she had been planning on for a while. Almost a year of his imprisonment, confusion, and dilemma. This was just his first test; he had passed it.

She could understand a part of the state of his mind. Questions, he would be tortured by the number of questions running through his mind. Why was he imprisoned? Why did she abduct him? Did she abduct him? What if she herself was in danger? What did she want from him? *All in good time you will know*, she whispered to herself. The question that bothered her was, why he didn't attempt to escape? What was on his mind that made him return? She reviewed the options in her head, but simply couldn't put a finger on a single one. Fingers crossed, she wanted to believe it was because of her—he respected her too much, or perhaps he felt sorry for her. She was even more afraid of the reason—what if it was her? It could flip either way. For now, she would slip quietly up the stairs and lock the door. Tomorrow, would be his second test.

Inside her soft baby pink quilt, she crawled in and inhaled her sweet-smelling baby lotion, and wriggled deeper under the blanket. It was a victory, although a tiny one. One that went to light up her night. Outside the window, the full moon beamed like a giant torch. The sky was cobalt blue; foggy skirt the air wore—something musical about it all she felt. Softly she hummed, whispering the words 'I will return—to Me.' Silence fell and the crickets stridulated and she fell asleep into the sweetest slumber.

Morning stringed into light with yellow streaks and purple dewdrops. The marigolds across the horizon were like large yellow polka dots. Jerry Mason did not sleep well last night. Recurring nightmares of his kidnapping, warped masked man dragging him through the window, his mouth gagged and eyes blindfolded—his struggle felt useless in comparison to that man who was almost twice his size. Disfigured, distorted images of the attic swam in front of him—sometimes enlarged in size, other times gobbling him like Pac-Man. He woke up with a throbbing headache, sweating, and deep dark circles under his eyes. The replay of the events of the night before punched him further down in spirits. He wished he had escaped; it was a moment of weakness that stood pulling him back in time and he surrendered.

He didn't know what today had in store for him. He had an uncanny feeling it wasn't going to be a regular day. *What of life that didn't slip in surprises like candies with explosively unexpected flavours, right?* He thought to himself, this solitary time with himself worked like therapy for him. He wondered when was the last time he had spoken to anyone. Months, maybe? There was a calendar in his attic, but he had lost track, and stopped turning the pages. One day, in his desperation, he turned it back to January. As if flipping those pages would bring him back the lost time. Roughly he could guess it was either end of November or early December.

December always smelled of Christmas—rich plum cakes, dry fruits soaked for months, sparkling lights, the vibrant colours. The spirit of Christmas penetrated even within the walls of an abandoned house. Charity to the needy, kindness to relatives, and the infectious feeling of simply being good. Christmas held warm memories for him. Mother's roast turkey and Macy's cherry chiffon cake. He wondered what his Christmas would be like this time. His thoughts were interrupted, he heard voices downstairs—not very clear, but he could distinguish them. So, there was more than one person today downstairs. He pressed his ears against the door to catch a phrase or two.

"Mrs. Davis, it is a pleasure to meet you once again. We wanted to speak with you for a bit, if you don't mind. We won't be long," Officer Scott stood at the door trying to peer inside.

"Officer Scott, am I right? Please come in. I wasn't expecting you, wish you would have informed me before coming. No worries, I can spare a few minutes," Mrs. Davis said, unsmilingly. Nervously following his gaze, she wondered what he was looking for.

"Thank you, Mrs. D. It is really an occupational hazard, that we have to arrive uninvited. I hope you can understand," Officer Scott said as he entered with his subordinate.

"Uh—oh, I understand. Tell me what it is that I can help you with."

"Actually, we were wondering if you could give us some insight into your family. As in who else is there in your family, or perhaps was in your family?"

"My family? My husband passed away twenty years back. We have lived here as long as I can remember since my marriage to my dearest Frank. All our relatives stay across the globe; none here, I am afraid. What may I ask has my lineage got to do with anything related to the police?"

"What about children? Did you have any? Are they perhaps abroad too?"

"I am afraid we were not blessed with any. Although Frank always wanted a boy. We tried… were unsuccessful, unfortunately," Mrs. Davis sniffed as her eyes filled with tears.

"Are you sure, Mrs. D, you didn't have a son working in the army? Take a look at this, it stands as proof of the same. I am confused, what would make you lie about your own son?" Scott whispered and poured some water for her, while the subordinate was busy taking notes, scribbling on a small notepad.

"I am sorry; I don't have any more time to talk to you. Please leave. I don't feel too well," said Mrs. Davis.

"Just one last question. The day before Jerry Mason's disappearance, did he come here to help you or meet you? How well did you know him, Mrs. D? What do you know about his disappearance?"

"I know nothing. He was just another neighbour's kid. He used to help everyone. I was no one special to him. Please kindly leave now," Mrs. D sounded exasperated.

Scott and his subordinate turned to leave, while Mrs. D followed them with her head bent down, sniffing softly. The police officers turned to leave and she bolted the door a little harder than necessary.

"She is blatantly lying to us," said Scott's subordinate Jack solemnly.

"I am so sure; what I don't understand is the reason. This changes everything. I mean why would she want to hide it? She is definitely hiding something. We need to dig deeper. If I hadn't known better, I would have easily fallen for that. It was pretty smooth."

Jerry Mason moved away from the door as he heard footsteps approaching the door. Impulsively, he dived behind the door and held a curtain rod in his hand—holding his breath. When the door opened, ever so little, he slid the rod in the nick of time and hit the person on the head. The body fell forward flat on the face—unconscious. He was stricken by what lay unconscious in front of him.

* * *

Earlier, this was not something Polly Mason may have even noticed. Sometimes, life has a way of teaching you things in a way that you may not perceive appropriate. Perhaps, one may even call it rather harsh, sardonic, brutal. Ironically, we can never take life to court and prove it unfair; such is the design of it. Polly Mason was peeping through the window to check if Jack had returned from work—wondering why he was so late tonight. She also had no clue where Macy was. It was after dark already; she should have been back from Helen's place. Last night she had taken her permission to study together with her school friend. Even then, Polly found it strange—she was not the type to study together, never had been. She surprised herself by consenting to it. Only later did she realise that she had agreed to let her go because she was feeling sorry for her little girl—what with her brother's disappearance, she was more lost, aloof, and anxious all the time.

Her heart broke every time she thought about their sibling bond. With Jerry's disappearance, it was like her Macy too had been lost. They had such a strong one, it made her proud. Sometimes, she would watch them quietly while they camped on the terrace, sharing dinner, Jerry telling her stories and Macy watching him adoringly, never once blinking, absorbing it all hungrily. Their laughter rang, echoed in her ears and she smiled while she was drenched in these memories; a sound shoved her out of it. Crashing back into reality, she noticed something odd at Mrs. Davis's house. Two police officers were leaving the house on their bike.

She found it strange that they were at Mrs. D's house. Why, she wondered would they be interrogating her feeble old friend? What could they want with her? What if she was in some problem? Thieves? Burglars? Could be anything? During her bad times she had been there for her family, she remembered that. If today she could be there for Mrs. D, she would do anything to help her out. These thoughts morphed her into severe panic mode and she ran to get her cell phone and call Mrs. D. No response. She kept on trying, with no luck. Her panic attack only became worse. Fingers fumbled on the phone as she pushed the keys harder, and her body started shaking back and forth on the chair. She did not feel well, her palms were sweaty and she was feeling unusually warm. Taking off her blue cardigan, she decided to take her medicine and lie down for some time. Terrible thoughts travelled through her mind. With her eyes closed tight she covered herself with her blanket. For a while, until the medicine started calming her nerves, she whimpered like a wounded kitten, short spasmodic shudders running through her.

It was only after that, that her breathing became rhythmic and she fell asleep finally. She woke up in the middle of the night—someone was shaking her softly. She woke up reluctantly. Sitting beside her, kneeling on the floor was her boy Jerry—untarnished, angelic, smiling at her with tears running down his cheeks as she cupped his face and he put his hands over hers. Violently she pulled him into her arms and crushed him into her chest. She wasn't going to let him go ever. In her arms, she would cradle him right here—protect him from whatever evil came his way. Yes, she was determined to fight anyone and everyone.

"Mama, I am here, I have always been here. Please don't worry about me. Please tell Dad I love him. Don't look for me anymore. It will hurt me if you do," Jerry whispered slowly, interrupted by hiccups filled with emotions.

"What are you talking about, Jerry? I am never letting you go. Shush, everything is alright now. I will take care of you," Polly whispered into his ears, as his warmth spread through her body like an antidote for all her pain and suffering.

"I can't Mama, I must go now. You will always be right in front of my eyes. I can't promise you I can come again. Maybe, one day I will return—to me," Jerry whispered, pecked her on both her cheeks and stared at her hard as if memorising this moment forever.

Immediately darkness fell like a thick curtain, paralysing Polly's vision ruthlessly. Her cry was like that of an animal caged, tortured, hysterical. Exhausted, her screams receded, alone she found herself once again. Crouched beside her bedside table, she fell unconscious to the world around her—head bent on her knees. In her mind she fought, I must not succumb, I will not fail. I will find him and rescue him. These three sentences she kept repeating to herself. Until they became softer, fainted into a silent oblivion, faded behind the facade of time.

No doors creaked, no cars honked, and no loud voices interrupted the night that had cascaded down so majestically.

There was silence—a thickness around it; impenetrable. Something sinister lay low, watching intently—daring the silence to crack. The streaks of innocence thinned, paled, weakened under its clutches. Hope was abandoned in the hands of a serrated, two-pronged road. Like a carcass it was exhibited—as if a thing unknown, a strange specimen left to be experimented upon—that none were ready to feel anymore, taste any longer, or dare to wear hope even.

It was a time to thrust the unsettled and the uncertain into the cavity that it had escaped from. Someone decided to do just that tonight. The Redbarrow Woods smelled of invasion tonight, rustling leaves, the soft crunch of berry shrubs, a trail of dense droplets of red. Something being dragged profusely heavy, heavy breathing with muffled groans. Suddenly the dragging stopped and a sharp penetration of a spade, scooping up murky mud continued for a long while. The hole got bigger, the sighs got heavier, until the motion stopped abruptly. Shoved inside that hole was a heavy load that fell with a loud thud. Mud was thrown back into the cavity rigorously until it levelled with the ground. Heavy footsteps receded from the woods until they became faint, faded into the highway, and an engine vroomed past its guilt.

Jack Mason parked his car and ran onto his porch; all the time his thoughts were occupied with his wife. Polly must be worried sick, his phone had died on him and he couldn't inform her that an unexpected meeting had come up for which he had to make a presentation like yesterday. In his mind, he was framing his apology as he tried to put the key inside the keyhole, and found the door slightly ajar. The apology fizzled out and he was alert as he tiptoed inside the house. He wondered if he should call the cops and report a break-in. Although he was sceptical about whether it was really a break-in, or perhaps Polly or Macy forgot to shut the door. On tiptoes, he crossed the living room. First, he softly opened Macy's door. The lights were out and she was completely under her duvet. A small sigh, at least his daughter was safe. Crossing the kitchen, he noticed nothing amiss. Finally, he went inside their bedroom—the lights were out and he found Polly crouched in the bedside corner, softly snoring.

Chapter 22

Nothing Fits

By the time I got home, it was already eight o'clock. I was petrified that they would interrogate and admonish me. Come to think of it, I have never done this before—being out for a night like this. Last night held one of those things that I simply couldn't put off. It never really occurred to me that rebellion, defiance, boldness would make me feel so delirious with excitement. It tasted cold and creamy like my first ice cream lick—almost immediately I knew, I was going to be addicted to trying it all over again. Freedom this was, it smelled of waves crashing on the shoreline—the salty residue leaving a coating on the nose. I didn't really plan it actually, things happened so fast, I could hardly resist, you see. If you were here, perhaps I could never have pulled it off. Without being cynical, I want to call it my lucky night.

I entered the house expecting Dad to see me from the dining room. Nothing seemed touched there. He walked out of his room, jumping on one foot wearing a sock, his tie hanging around his collar. He gave me a puzzled look, not an angry one.

"Since when do you go for a walk in the mornings? Not that I am complaining, exercise is always good for the mind and body. Just pleasantly surprised seeing you at it," Dad smiled.

"Umm... yes, I have been thinking about your advice to exercise for a while now. Early morning today, I decided to give it a go. It sure does feel good," I said smiling back, trying to sound as convincing as possible.

"Proud of you, my girl. I am in a terrible hurry today, will leave now. Your mother, she doesn't seem well, I am afraid. Keep an eye on her today, please. Last night, when you came, did you leave the door open by any chance? I have to say, that is very careless of you, Mace, what with all the deaths and the kidnappings," Dad scolded me.

"Oh! I must have been really tired, don't really remember doing that though. Are you sure it was not a burglar or an intruder? Sure, I will take care of Mama. Let me quickly pack something for you to eat on the way," I said.

This piece of news took me by surprise. Who could it be, I wondered. Dad mentioned he didn't see anything missing, which further piqued my interest. I packed him some sandwiches, a couple of apples, and a big flask of tea. He bickered, and fussed, but in the end, he took it all with him.

After taking a shower and making my bed, exhaustion swamped me into a dreamless slumber. When I woke up, the sky seemed like a thick froth of grey clouds—like eyes filled with tears. This is the thing with winters; you can never tell the time simply by looking at the sky. It just always looks cosy, and lazy, and seduces you to sleep some more. I lifted myself onto the bed with one eye closed to check the time; it was half past four. Jumping out of bed, I decided to check on Mama. On entering the room, I was greeted by an empty bed and a vacant room. Not very far away, I could hear the shower running in the bathroom. The room looked untidy—an unmade bed, too many pills on Mama's bedside table, the dressing table had too much clutter, bottles of body lotion, perfumes, foundations, lipsticks rolled open, five different combs and brushes scattered one over the other. Then, I noticed something on the floor. Before I could pick it up and take a closer look at it, Mama came out of the bathroom.

She jumped back on seeing me—frightened as if I was an intruder. I held her by her shoulders and made her sit. She looked at me with more focus and her shoulders slumped. I felt a deep gash, slit, crack within me somewhere, seeing this woman, who has tirelessly brought us up, and now, after you being gone, it feels like she is working on one limb only. Instinctively, I gave her a tight hug—filling her with wordless gratitude. Even though most days I may find myself in the neglected category, yet I know now, I understand the effort she has put into bringing us up. She didn't return my hug for a few seconds, every bone in her body tense, alert, resisting me. Suddenly she broke open, speaking too fast in whispers. It all sounded gibberish to me. I wondered what had upset her so much. She continued this every few minutes, her pace fluctuating. I tried to calm her down, without jerking her out of it too hard.

"Mama... calm down, please talk a little slower. I cannot understand anything. Are you not feeling well? Maybe we should visit the doctor, let me call and make an appointment," I said.

She pulled me back.

"No, I don't need the doctor. He came last night, Mace, we need to help him, he is in trouble. My poor boy! He was saying some strange things, he looked different too—like he was working out. His body was toned, hair has grown long, that hollowness, loneliness inside him was like a parasite eating him from inside. I just wanted to hold him in my embrace and keep him away from all those ugly monsters out there. I don't know what to do, I feel so helpless, Mace," she started weeping again.

"I don't understand, Mama, who came? What are you talking about? You must have had a bad dream. Please just calm down, I'll get you some water. You lie down, everything is perfectly alright," I said and ran into the kitchen to get a glass of water. I opened the fridge and was filling a glass with water, when I accidentally caught a glimpse of a shadow standing right behind me.

"It was not a dream; you don't believe me? He was here, he came to meet me. I touched his face, the warmth of it still tingles on

my palm. He said he is right here, he will always be watching me," Mama said in a monotone as if she had been hypnotised. I fumbled with the glass, and a few drops fell out before I was able to grip it. Nothing fitted. Common sense tells me, this is all in her head. Her tone, it scrapes the nape of my conscience. Yet there is an itch I can't ignore, what if she is telling the truth? The more I say it to myself, the sillier I feel. I gave her the glass of water and busied myself in the kitchen. It felt imperative that I should call the doctor and make an appointment, so I excused myself; I couldn't do it in front of her, it might agitate her, so in my room behind closed doors I made an appointment with the doctor for a slot tomorrow.

Cooking has always helped me in seeing sense, so I took refuge in this haven. Mama for the time being sipped her water and was silent for a while. I planned to make something that would demand all my concentration—my undivided attention; that way I could stop these random thoughts from festering fear inside me. My choices narrowed down to good old Shepherd's Pie for supper, and for dessert, I planned on making apple strudel. I watched the mince thaw under the running water in the sink, while mother's words kept running through my head—like headlines playing repetitively on the news channel. As much as I tried to ignore it, it all went in vain. Meticulously, I diced the vegetables.

The smell of caramelising onions in the pan helped in distracting my array of worries, at least for the moment. The ground meat sizzled in its juices with the tinted golden onions; the sound reminded me of the rains two years back, continuous and very heavy. At night all four of us would huddle together, drinking hot cocoa and you reading aloud John Keats. I liked to close my eyes and imagine 'A Thing of Beauty' one of my favourite poems. The dried parsley, thyme, rosemary, salt, and pepper married the flavours of the meat with its juices. I let it get slightly caught at the bottom—the unburnt burnt texture accentuates the flavours just moments before

I dashed in Worcestershire Sauce and garlic. The spices sang and wafted around the house like merry lights. A thing of beauty indeed is the art of cooking. Layering the meat under the mashed potatoes, I slipped it into the oven.

We were happy, I agree, thinking back about those days. The thing about life is, it is a wreath made of deeds, decisions, and death. There is no return, only repentance before the finality of death. The sooner we figure and stop deceiving ourselves, the better it is for us. I moved on to the apple strudel. Once the dough sat tight in a corner resting, I chopped the apples into batonnet size and spiced it up with golden raisins and apple juice. I was almost done, when the door opened and Dad walked back in. Mama also came outside to greet him; I could only pray she didn't start her rant all over again. Dad didn't need it; he already looked so exhausted after work.

"I saw two cops at Mrs. Davis's house yesterday. I wonder why they were visiting her. Strange," Mama said during dinner. This is new, she didn't mention this to me, I thought to myself uncomfortably. I refrained from reacting, instead decided to listen to them passively, while I scooped up a spoonful of my pie.

"Is that so? I hope she is all right, Polly. You should call her and check on her. The dear old lady has always been so helpful to us. Perhaps, we can help her out?" Dad suggested.

"I did call. The strange thing is she didn't answer her phone then and she is still not answering her phone. I am starting to get worried about her. What should we do? We must do something, right?" Mama said with a frown on her forehead. Suddenly she looked so much older than she actually is. This bit of information got me worried too. Where was all this coming from? What in God's name was going on? I was unable to fathom.

"Are you sure? This is getting weirder and weirder. We should inform the police, then. After dinner, I will call the Chief and tell him to check it out," Dad decided.

"What if her phone died, or something? Why bother the cops without checking out ourselves? I can drop in at her place tomorrow and confirm if everything is fine. If not, then we can call the cops tomorrow?" I piped in quickly. I needed to do this without anyone else's involvement.

"That does make sense, wise little owl you have grown into. Do that first thing in the morning and then we can take a call. You want me to come with you?"

"No! I can go myself; I am not a baby, Dad."

"All right, don't get all adult on me now. Just be careful."

All the information unloaded unsettled me a lot. Inside my room after dinner, I paced around the room. If she wasn't lying about that, then maybe... I was frightened to even frame the doubt in my head. Did you really come here? Suddenly I felt very cold, my window was open and the chill gnawed at my skin. I recoiled with my back against the window, when I felt eyes on me, like I was being watched. With a jerk I turned to look—a black cat with green eyes menacingly meowed at me from the window sill. Crossly, I strode towards it—daring it to come inside. I banged the windows shut and she jumped outside.

The sky shed off her night skin and donned a piercingly purple tinge in the morn. I woke up abruptly hearing the cars honking loudly. Outside, Mama was in the kitchen making breakfast—physically there, mentally she seemed too far away. I greeted her with a kiss on the cheek. She mumbled "Jerry..." turning towards me, then the light in her eyes faded seeing me. Perhaps on a usual day, it would have offended me, but not today—I had too much on my mind. After breakfast, I ventured out to go and check on Mrs. Davis, like I said I would. On my bicycle, I reached there within a few minutes. Usually, around this time of the day, Mrs. Davis waters the plants or sits outside with her letter pad, but today I didn't see her. Odd.

Once I reached the porch, I rang the bell. No answer. I tried at least four times, before something actually felt wrong there. I saw a pair of muddy shoes—there was fresh mud on them and that's not all, they didn't look like Mrs. D's shoes at all. These were brown leather ones, with thick, sturdy soles—men's shoes. I didn't know what to make of this, I panicked. After another ten minutes, I screamed for Mrs. Davis, standing right outside the door. Nothing. I found myself thinking of ways to break inside the house. I was too frightened to try something so adventurous within the span of twenty-four hours of my escapade.

I resigned from this assignment and decided to return home. There was nothing much I could do. If she was in real trouble, we needed to get the police involved. I called Dad immediately and informed him. Within ten minutes, I heard the police sirens buzzing down our neighbourhood. By this time, I was back at home, and Mama and me watched through the window—just like the rest of our nosy neighbours. From our window though, we could get a clear view of Mrs. Davis's house. They broke open the door and a handful of armed cops entered the house—like invading a terrorist's house. We waited for something new, for what seemed like hours, but nothing happened. Finally, the Chief came out with Officer Scott—there was no sign of Mrs. Davis.

"They didn't find her, poor Mrs. D. What did they do to her? She was such a kind soul," Mama cried clutching the curtain.

"I am sure the cops will find her, Mama; don't you get yourself worked up about it."

I knew they would not find her; I was pretty sure of it. Yet, I didn't know how I was so definite about it, it troubled me.

"Just like they found Jerry and the identity of that dead body?"

I winced inwardly; the fact was we had all lost hope. The police had disappointed us all the time. The mysteries were just piling up and none had been solved yet. Nothing definite or concrete had been disclosed to us so far. It was hard to believe we would be able to find her too. Suddenly, there was a lot of movement, the cops seemed to have found something. There was excitement and sniffer dogs were called in to snoop around. My hands felt clammy and I didn't feel well at all. So, I told Mama, I was going to rest inside and left.

Chapter 23

Tracking Mrs. Davis

The small town of Redbarrow Woods was filmed with a thin crust of ice all over from the streets up into the woods. Ice has a frigid way of penetrating—cutting deep within the soul, it slithers mutely with a purpose. At first, it feels easy to combat it—wrestle it out with a jumper, for just the initial few days. Over time though, delicate layers overlap one over the other, and become a stronger army. Such was the state in this neighbourhood. A humming buzz of a monstrosity infected the minds, and fear generated from the soles travelled into the nerves of the brain. Disappearances that occurred seemed never to be reversed. At the heart of this very city, the palpitations droned getting only louder with time. A restlessness that damped, jarred, and stunted hope sprayed on everyone's faces.

People stopped venturing out at night, frightened of the unseen. Who would be the next victim was the bet on—first a lad, then an old lady, who next? Who was doing this? Was it an animal? Those old legends creeped out about the woods. The elders believed, narrated in deep, gruff, resounding voices—the inevitable was here to stay. They said there would be more. It was hungry now; someone had woken up the beast of the Redbarrow Woods. It would come in different forms and taste the blood of the young and the old. It stirred the air—a haunting feel that drowned all measures of forbearance. What of life if it doesn't feel threatened time and again—an old drunkard sang swaying on the empty desolate streets of the terrified city.

It folded incongruously all the good spirit. A thin sliver would peep every now and then, only to be gorged away by the acidic greyness that shadowed the days and nights. There was no sweetness this holiday season, a bitter aftertaste coated the palate of celebrations. No carols tempered it any happier, lights flickered ominously. People were growing anxious and more agitated by the helplessness of the situation. This was not a wait-and-watch game they wanted to play. Their demand—that law and order be restored, the feeling of safety that they starved for was unnerving.

The cops seemed to be in an un-news state. They simply remained silent; no comments ever were heard from them. They would simply hum and buzz around the station. Word was out that they were on the verge of cracking the case of disappearances. None really believed it, that was the only thing everyone was heard talking about these days. When will they do the big reveal? Would an official statement be released or a press conference would be held before the year-end?

December was like the bell that rang at the end of a period at school. It was expected to be shrill—alerting everybody far and wide that it was about to move from a comma to a full stop. Decisions to be made, wrapping up the pending logs from the year around. The layers of dust to be broomed away, so that it could pave way for new beginnings. Unfortunately, not everyone's December ends with a clean slate like that. Some arrive abruptly on a halt called death. This year too ended for some with undefined definitions. Those whom they left behind were stuck between hell and paradise.

At least a dozen officers were searching the woods, wearing heavy overcoats and boots. Sniffer dogs were getting close—they were excited and started barking loudly. Chief Grant and Officer

Scott moved ahead of the crowd to look at what was being dug out. It was not a pretty sight. After hours of digging, no body was found. The biting cold wave dithered ever so strongly. The hours stretched like an evening shadow on the prowl. After searching Mrs. Davis' house, the cops found a number of clues that led to the woods. There were three sets of footprints—the leather shoes with a fresh coat of mud from these very woods. There were marks of blood—like those of a body being dragged from the attic to the living room. The attic looked lived in, fingerprints were found on the desk and chair, and the bed had a pillow with the soft dent of a head. The smell of sweat mixed with some fragrance of baby lotion was pronounced. There was no old man found—as Mrs. Davis had mentioned to Officer Scott.

The immediate need of the hour, was to find the body—if there was one. The traces of a body being buried were prominent, the dogs had smelled it too—blood stains on a peach-coloured bedsheet that had been used and left there. It was around three when the search widened. The team of officers looked exhausted and the dogs were too. Darkness fell with a masked intensity; the woods were never lit for reasons of preserving the natural environment. With the winter high into the act—a gush of fog invaded the woods too. Obscurity shook all sense of reasoning; fatigue dragged the search into an abyss from which there simply seemed no way out. It was a labyrinth that never spelt exit. They were far deeper into the midst of the wilderness than they could have estimated. It was like a jungle of moss furnaces; only they were frozen fumes of ice breathing in them. It was almost six in the morning when Chief Grant decided that it was time to return. They would have to come back another day or perhaps they would have to look elsewhere.

While the cops receded out of the woods, not very far away, crouched high up on a thick branch, someone let out a heavy sigh. Officer Scott stopped in his tracks instinctively and took a good look around. Nothing stirred. He shook his head and believed it was merely his imagination and sprinted to catch up with his team. The leaves rustled, a slight twitch—some movement of numb legs stretching out just to yawn out the creases. Muffled groans escaped piercing through the stillness of dawn. Sunlight paled on the yellowish-green leaves; a sweet smell of lavender percolated through the air. The musty heaviness of anxiety lifted off like a veil from the shadowed night. Wrapped in a thick blanket was bearded Jerry Mason with almost purple lips, teeth chattering an unmusical tone, toes and fingers numb from the cold. Next to him, wrapped in a thicker blanket lay another body. Lifelessly still, it lay bundled up tightly, and Jerry hugged it tightly. He gripped it tight in one hand and climbed down the sturdy old oak tree. The branches whispered soft notes; it was as if they were whispering soft words of sorrow, pain, and strength to Jerry.

The numbness heightened Jerry's feeling of disorientation. He couldn't understand where he could go to find help or why he was doing this even. For a long time, he walked around in circles around the tree, laying the body on the ground. Every few minutes he checked the pulse and breath. The pulse knocked irregularly as if it was fighting for life. He didn't have time at all, he knew that. Who could he go to, who would let him in, without questioning the life out of him? Home? The thought didn't seem like a solution; he was surprised at that. Home would have to wait. He thought about everyone, and he knew the answer finally. Negative came the answer. Suddenly, he remembered somebody he had a feeling would help him without badgering him down. He didn't have any other choice; he had to trust his gut.

He had no money on him, the distance was too long, and he had to take a cab. After half an hour, he finally saw a cab coming his way. The cab driver looked at Jerry suspiciously—and rightly so because he did look like a runaway fugitive.

"Please, my mother is not well, I need to get her help as soon as possible, otherwise it will be too late. Please give us a ride, we have been waiting for the longest time. No other cabs came this way."

"I am sorry, this looks like a police case, I don't want to be involved in all this. Please take another cab."

"You will not get into any trouble. I beg of you. What if she was your mother? Would you have left her to die like this?"

The cab driver harrumphed and eventually agreed to drop them off. The journey seemed longer than it actually was. When the thread of life is about to tear, it usually feels so. Finally, they reached the house by the sea. The only house he believed the police wouldn't be patrolling. The sun was escaping beyond the horizon just as they got out of the car. The house was well lit up by lamps on the porch. Not a soul was around the beach. Jerry asked the cab to wait and ran inside to get the money. He rang the bell. No answer. He rang it again. This time the lock turned and someone opened the door.

A frighteningly charged undercurrent passed between the two people staring at each other. Ms. Mary removed her glasses to wipe them again, because she simply couldn't believe who was standing in front of her. Jerry Mason looked at her and immediately fell into her arms.

"Jerry, is that really you? Oh, my dear boy, I was so worried about you," Ms. Mary hugged him back tightly, her voice overwhelmed with emotions.

"Ms. Mary, please help me. I need some money; the cab is waiting outside."

She ran inside to get her purse and gave him the change immediately. Jerry gave the money to the driver and carried the body inside.

"What's happening, Jerry, who is this? Is this a dead body? Oh, what have you done, Jerry? This is not good. Not good at all. I need to call the cops."

"Ms. Mary, please, we need a doctor as soon as possible. No, this is not a dead body. This is Mrs. Davis; she is still alive. She is my neighbour—lives in house number 46. We need to get her warm. I didn't know where else to go. Please don't call the police yet. I need a few answers; then I promise I will call the cops myself."

"I don't understand, Jerry. If you say so, I'll call my family doctor. In the meantime, take her inside and put her on the bed and cover her with blankets," Ms. Mary found herself agreeing to his requests even though she didn't have a very good feeling about this.

Inside the house, with the heater on and blankets covering Mrs. Davis, colour was coming back into her cheeks. Within an hour, the doctor arrived. A short, stout old man who had kind eyes, he walked in and immediately attended to Mrs. Davis.

"I have plastered all the visible wounds. Her vitals look all right for right now, but due to a lot of blood loss, she is very weak. Needs a lot of liquids and fruits. Please arrange for saline bottles regularly. I have attached one as of now. She needs complete rest. She should gain consciousness soon. If there is anything else, please give me a call."

"Thank you so much, doctor. You truly are a lifesaver," Ms. Mary smiled at him.

After the doctor left, Ms. Mary hurried into the kitchen to prepare food while Jerry had a bath and kept a watch on Mrs. Davis. By the time they sat down to eat, Jerry was famished and gobbled up the food. Ms. Mary nibbled on the food and watched him eat. To her, all this felt almost unreal. She pinched herself to believe that after all those months of praying, Jerry

Mason was actually sitting in front of her tonight. She offered up a silent prayer of gratitude. Although she had tonnes of questions to ask him, she saw the fatigue in his body language and his eyes. So, she decided her questions could wait. What the boy really needed now was the rest after all that he must have gone through. One pertinent question kept nudging her though. Why did he not go home, and instead he came to her for help? Surely, he felt safe at home?

After food, Jerry slept through the afternoon and they had a light early dinner in the evening. They spent an uneventful night; Ms. Mary slept with Mrs. Davis and kept checking on her, while Jerry slept in the guest room. He offered to keep watch on her, but she insisted he needed the rest just as much. In the end, he agreed, and the moment his head touched the pillow, he sank into a deep, dreamless slumber after almost a year. In the morning when he woke up, sunlight poured luxuriously into his room, and the soft sound of the sea waves filtered in, bringing him back to where he was. He woke up with a throbbing head; there was so much he needed to do. He needed to give answers to Ms. Mary, he needed to get answers himself. On that thought, he jumped out of bed to check on Mrs. Davis.

Mrs. Davis was sitting inclined on two pillows, sipping tea and looking outside the window, when Jerry walked in. He saw a thin stream of tears running down her eyes—no expression, an innate sadness that could sting anyone who even looked at her, and there was something else in those eyes—it was sort of a flicker of something odd—he simply couldn't place a finger on it. When he entered the room, slowly she moved her face to look into his eyes. Looking at him, it was like she was pleading with him for something; an apology? Why—her face was contorted with emotions. Unrestrained, the tears started flowing and she started weeping uncontrollably. He ran inside to calm her down.

Putting the teacup down, she wept into his shirt—at first, it was just damp, but as time passed it became soaking wet. He was at a loss for words, he mumbled and tried to say it was okay, everything was all right now. But the words—they just wouldn't come out; he kept choking them back in. In reality, it was not fair, what had happened to him. Without knowing the reasons, he simply couldn't bring himself to console her verbally. As much as his kindness fought, somewhere in his heart, the agony inside was driving him insane and was winning the battle at that.

When Ms. Mary entered after a while, she turned pale—she saw Mrs. Davis stabbing Jerry repetitively with a syringe in her hand and she was screaming like a maniac. She was doing it with a maddening fervour—almost delicately, yet with so much menace and gore, it was the most abhorring sight she had ever witnessed in her life. She was confused, didn't understand what was happening. Was she hallucinating all this? She blinked her eyes twice and tried to erase the scene. Nothing changed. Jerry was struggling to fight her off, but so much blood had flowed that he became weak and limp to the point of unconsciousness, that he had no fight left in him.

"I am sorry, my son. It's time for you to go now. Sleep, my child, sleep tight."

She didn't even realise that Ms. Mary was staring at her from the door, paralysed by the scene.

Chapter 24

Mrs. Davis's Son

"Yes, I had a son in the army. His name was Sergeant Jeremy Davis. He was so handsome, that if you looked at him just once, you wouldn't have been able to take your eyes off him immediately. He rose in the ranks rapidly because of his bravery, skill, and strategic mind. The senior officers always raved about him, praising him and his dedication. He was loved by all. The juniors worshipped him and everyone always said he had a special glint in his eyes," Mrs. Davis gulped some tea before continuing.

"I used to write long letters to him. He loved reading my letters, you know. More than that I used to wait for his letters. He wrote such detailed letters; he would tell me about everything, the smallest of things that happened to him.

I don't remember when the nightmares started, I think it was after I moved here, The Redbarrow Woods. They made me anxious and I would sob through the night fearing for his life. I wrote to him even more frequently. Of course, I never did mention my fears to him, I didn't want him to be worried about me. He was too busy, he barely wrote back anymore, and when he did, his letters were too brief. This just added to my sorrow. I didn't have anywhere to go, no one to talk to about it. When your son decides to become a soldier, you have to accept that perhaps one day he might never return. What kind of mother can ever believe that completely, right?" She wiped away her tears and sighed with a lot of effort, while Jerry listened to her story intently. She continued.

"Then, one day he wrote that he was coming to visit me. I was ecstatic, so thrilled to read it. It washed away all my hiccups for a bit at least. I redecorated the house, hired a gardener to manicure the garden neatly, and made all his favourite dishes too. The day finally arrived, it was such a glorious, cheerful day—I still remember the golden fireball falling like a halo, pale, yet bright on the house and garden. It smelled of fennel, strawberries, and roses—like a potpourri, only it was simply the anticipation of my dear boy's return. I couldn't stop smiling from at least ten days before that day... my jaws still hurt even thinking about it. I waited and watched the sun sail across the horizon. No sign of my Jeremy. I hadn't even eaten lunch. Thought I would eat with him. He never did come.

I wrote him a letter the next day; no reply ever came back. Then a few days later I had visitors—two army officers came by. They said he was missing in action. I was angry with them, so angry. How dare they say such things? Did they not know how good he was? The reality was that such things happened all the time and most of them are presumed dead. Not my Jerry, not even for one second, could I believe that he could be lost or he would meet death so early. I simply couldn't bring myself to believe that. My promising, valiant, resilient son—a soldier who everyone imagined would die defending his country, had left us in such an abrupt way.

So, I subconsciously refused to believe it—simply blocked it in. I waited for him, yearned for him. Months passed. I heard nothing. Then one night I heard a soft rap on my door. In that least-expected moment, I found him on my porch. There was a thick vagueness around him. He was very sick— couldn't get out of bed. The fever never seemed to give way for months. His body couldn't take it; slowly, limb by limb it started disintegrating. I didn't lose hope, at least he was with me. No one in this neighbourhood knew about him, none at all—no wait—except for the postman, Mr. Parker, a very kind man.

One fine day, maybe two years later, he started looking like himself. Rapidly his strength came back. As he got healthier, his mind became restless. He wanted to return to the army. Every day we would fight about it. I couldn't bear the thought of losing him again. He tried to coax me, convince me, even pleaded desperately. What kind of assurance was he trying to make me buy, I failed to understand? The daily drill compelled me to do something rash. I hatched a plan. In my desperation, I resorted to what was unimaginable to any mother.

I decided to hire a nurse—who would attend to his every need. I sold this proposition to him saying that on the condition that he got completely better, I would perhaps consider his decision. To this, he agreed immediately. I was elated. Now, it was time to ignite the fire. I instructed the nurse to keep him drugged—so he always felt sleepy, tired, and out of breath. This carried on for months— his spirit was spent; he had no willpower left in him anymore. In my greed to keep him near me, I never realised how far I was sending him away. Until one day, the inevitable happened. He had managed to persuade the nurse to tell him the truth. Then they conspired on a plan for his escape and one morning he was simply gone forever.

You see, my mind was not the same, not after losing my boy. He was my life, after all. So, I continued to write letters to him—for many months or years maybe, even now, at times I am tempted to write a letter to him. The reason is simple, that was my last link to him—it was my only connection to him for the longest time. Writing letters somehow keeps him for me forever. It never occurred to me even once that there was something absurd in doing this," Mrs. Davis dabbed her tears with a towel and sipped some tea before continuing.

"Then one day, I noticed you for the first time. It was like an awakening; a second chance life was blessing me with. Have you ever had your deepest wish granted? You were mine. At first, I couldn't believe my eyes. For months I watched you, tried to make conversation with you. Tried to gauge your temperament. It was unbelievable, how easy you were—so warm, kind, and strikingly similar. I wrote about you too, in my letters, describing my joy on your discovery. I couldn't share it with anyone, you see, none at all. You started visiting me more frequently—I made up desperate excuses to bring you home. My hunger to have you stay in my place grew almost monstrous—I cooked your favourite dishes; they were not the same as his though. I gave you presents. Just look at the coincidence that your names were also the same.

I even befriended your mother, father, and sister, just so I could be close to you. In reality, I never really liked them. For you, what extent I could have gone, you don't have any idea. Or perhaps, now you do. No one suspected my intentions; I tried my level best to conceal my immense ecstasy. Then one day, I found a way to make you mine forever. It was a slip-up on my side, it turned out just perfect, you see? I am tired now; I have told you too much for your own good. I don't know why I felt the need to explain all this to you. You saved my life; I will always owe that to you. You have become too dangerous. If you tell the cops, I won't have anywhere to go."

After saying all this to Jerry, Mrs. Davis started attacking him. Jerry was taken completely by surprise. He struggled in shock, unable to retaliate or save himself. He was so engrossed in her story that he simply couldn't imagine something like this happening to him.

"Please, Mrs. Davis, don't do this. Why now? After all that has happened, I will not tell the police anything, I promise," Jerry pleaded helplessly.

He was surprised at how strong she actually was. What scared him the most was her strange manic, roving eyes. At this point, Ms. Mary witnessed the scene from outside and became petrified, and frozen into immobility, so great was the shock of it. She didn't know what to do. Eventually, out of desperation, she sneaked in behind Mrs. Davis and banged her head with a large vase. Mrs. Davis collapsed on the ground and Ms. Mary ran to Jerry. He lay unconscious and bleeding. She managed to fumble with her phone and dialled for the ambulance and then the cops.

* * *

The small hospital room was packed with flowers and get well soon cards. There were two plastic chairs on one side of the room that were used by two police officers, on the other side there was a small table with two cell phones, one on charge, and the other blinking a blue light. Next to it was a brown leather couch-cum-bed. Mrs. and Mr. Mason sat on it—their heads bent low. The light on the machine attached to the patient beeped rhythmically and their eyes kept darting from the patient to the machine. Mr. Mason stood up to stroll and stretch his legs a bit, while Mrs. Mason stood by the bed and put her hand gently on the patient's forehead. For the umpteenth time, she did that so she could believe her own eyes. Finally, her darling son was back. But the situation in which they received him was such that they didn't know whether to celebrate or to mourn. The doctors said that if he had been brought even slightly later, it would have been too late. They said, at least for another forty-eight hours, he had to be kept under observation.

Polly had hugged and thanked Ms. Mary for managing to call the police on time, putting her own life at risk. She said she would forever be indebted to her for it. Ms. Mary was in a state of shock when she was brought into the hospital. The doctor said she would also need to spend the night at the hospital. She was an old lady and this kind of shock was not good for her heart. They sedated her—so she could get proper rest. As for Mrs. Davis, she was also admitted to the hospital; due to her poor health, there were two guards kept outside her room and Officer Scott was waiting too. They had found enough proof from her place to accuse her of kidnapping and attempted murder. Yet, there were many loopholes that still needed untangling.

Officer Scott stood outside the hospital room, staring through the window. It had been a long day. He turned to check on Mrs. Davis lying on the bed. Until she gained consciousness, there wasn't much he could do. Jerry Mason had returned from the dead, which was a relief. It was clear now, that she had hired someone to kidnap him. The cops had found all her letters and the motive was clear too. She had lost her son and she saw her son in Jerry. The dead body they had found had also been identified as that of Sergeant Jeremy Davis—her runaway son. After abandoning his mother, Jeremy Davis's condition had worsened, and eventually, his mental health kept him from leading a normal life. He became addicted to drugs and eventually he was killed for not being able to pay for them. Officer Scott had a strong hunch there was something or someone else at play in all this. He just couldn't figure out who it was yet. Officer Scott spent the night in the hospital in Mrs. Davis's room to ensure the safety of the accused.

"Scott, there is a huge gap in this story, according to Ms. Mary's statement. Jerry had rescued Mrs. Davis, then the question is who had buried her, that too alive? What is going on in that house, I fail to understand. You need to get to the bottom of all this. I must say, your postman Mr. Parker was a good lead. Keep up the good work!" Chief Grant said to Scott.

"Thank you, Chief. Learning from the best, after all. I will get to the bottom of this by tomorrow."

In the morning he reported back to the station to discuss things with the chief. The station was buzzing with rumours about the case and its new developments. The reporters outside waited like predators hungry for a story to polish off. The fact that Jerry Mason had returned from the dead, had shone a good light on the cops. The small town of Redbarrow Woods suddenly felt safer and the residents were singing high praise for the cops. However, the scene into the investigation was far from over. It was getting more intense than ever before.

"I had a restless night thinking about the missing equation in this story. There is another accomplice free and roaming around in the city. It is not safe to leave either the accused or the victim without constant protection. The confusion, Chief, is whether it was an accomplice or maybe another individual entity altogether. If the person was an accomplice, why would they attempt to kill Mrs. Davis? That is the question that nags me the most. I am pretty sure whoever it is, is a professional at this game. Someone cold, ruthless, and calculative—the kind that buries people alive. It sends shivers down my spine to even think about it. The more I think about the case, the more it seems to get complicated."

"Scott, I don't understand the dynamics between Mrs. Davis and Jerry Mason—first she gets him kidnapped and imprisons him for months in that attic. Then, someone tries to kill her and buries her alive. Next, Jerry rescues her and endangers his own life to save hers? To top it off, Mrs. Davis after recovering, attacks the person who saved her? What if Jerry Mason is in fact not telling the truth, after all?" Chief Grant lit another smoke and puffed it with a sigh. Officer Scott was more than confused now.

"Are you trying to say, that perhaps, Jerry is not all that innocent? He was the one who attempted to kill her and she knew this, so she attempted to kill him? Chief, why would he bury her and save her at the same time? Something doesn't fit. I don't know what it is. I am going to go back to the hospital and check on Mrs. Davis and get a statement from that boy too."

"Perhaps he panicked when he heard the siren? No, not possible to do the digging and the exhuming so quickly. We are clearly missing something here. Keep me posted Scott, and just keep an eye out for any unusual, strange visitors. Next time I hear from you, I want to hear the end of this. Completely flat out in the open."

* * *

When I woke up, there was a stagnancy in the air. Have you ever felt like the end was near? I could smell it on me and everywhere around me. No, not death—that would be far too easy, it was a finish line of sorts. My dark secrets; I could feel them being ripped apart from me and each one fell on the ground—like a string of pearls had been snatched from my neck. It was loud, and clumsy. Each pearl fell with a thud on the ground. The walls were greyish black—not freshly painted—it was scaling away in chunks. My hair was all dishevelled, my eyelashes had thick beads of tears on them, kohl-streaked cheeks, and my red lipstick smeared on the right-side jawline. I was in a long strappy black dress and an elegant pair of golden heels.

Where was I? It was a long room, some sort of a banquet hall—there were people with masks on. Everyone was staring at me—whispering, pointing, nudging each other about me. The funny thing was, even with the mask I could recognise each one of them—Mama, Dad, Mrs. Smith, Officer Scott, Chief Grant, my teachers, my friends—practically every soul that lived in our small town. Why? I screamed—held mother by her shoulders, shook her—she didn't react, simply stood and stared at me begrudgingly. I moved from person to person—none of them reacted to me. Then, I saw at the far end of the room, Mrs. Davis sitting on her knees, whimpering softly with her head on your lap—you were so still. I tried to read your expression. It was cold like a rock had been pulled out from the centre of the ocean. I wanted to believe I didn't understand any of this. Didn't I?

Everything fades rather obscurely—wildly things strobing in quick moves and I can feel someone shaking me vigorously. I open my eyes to Mama smiling and tears running down her cheeks. That was a dream, I sigh myself awake. I wonder what must have happened now, I simply cannot imagine. I wriggle up reluctantly and ask her.

"Mace! It's Jerry, they have found him and he is at the hospital. Dad and me have been there since last night. We didn't want to wake you up. I have come to take you now," Mama says, overjoyed.

Chapter 25

Macy

I hate that light falls, why won't it rise? Rather myopic, generic, and predictable it seems on its part. Mama is waiting outside; I am in my bathtub filled with bubbles—I swish it with my hands and twirl it with my toes. I feel as if a train is running inside me; no, I don't mean to stop it. My anxiety feels heightened, I want to hurry, make it faster, you see. I feel detached from the Macy everyone here knows; I don't understand me. Have you ever felt like that? Like there is a cold rush drenching inside me. A secret—a stranger I know, who whispers to me. I dip my full face and body inside the bathtub. The foggy thoughts are cut off, it's calm, so silent. I hold my breath back; eyes closed lightly. I wait there inside for a couple of minutes, daring myself to stretch my willpower to not give up. The body sends signals—the sudden urge to come out of it. I think to myself I should fight it just a tad bit longer. There is something so delicious in defying the odds in clandestine—don't you think? You were never like that, I know.

The bathroom door—I hear it bang loudly; although a slightly muffled sound. I jerk out of the water, gulping in the air in big gulps, wiping my face and trying to pacify my beating heart. This is the rush I have always enjoyed. Mama is screaming for me to hurry now. There is a part of me that is dying to see you—of course how can I not? So, I yell back I will be out in five. I scrub myself and wash, wrap the dressing gown, and come out. She's not in the room; I hear the pots and pans in the kitchen. I put on the first thing that comes into my hand, brush my hair back and tie it into a messy knot. Finally, I dab my face with some blush and kohl and sigh a little too loudly before leaving the room. Mama has prepared food and I see a casserole being sealed tightly.

When Officer Scott reached the hospital, he found a big crowd around Mrs. Davis's room. This didn't feel right—he sprinted and pushed himself through the crowd, flashing his badge. The doctor stopped him just as he was about to get a closer look at her.

"What… what is wrong, doctor? Is she all right? She is the prime accused in the case."

"Officer, please let me do my duty. She had a sudden attack, her blood pressure shot up. We are doing our best. I request you to please stand back and let us do our duty."

"All right, I will get out of your way. I need to keep officers on watch and I want this crowd gone. Her life might be in danger."

The doctor nodded and rattled at the increasing number of reporters to disperse and got back to attending to his patient. Scott murmured to himself 'not good' and strode away to check on Jerry. When he arrived, only Mr. Mason was there, sitting with his head on the sofa. He looked tired and even older. Scott felt sorry for the father; a mammoth episode of a son can surely make a man fragile and disheartened, he thought to himself. Still, at least he had got his son back alive. When he approached the nurse attending to Jerry, Mr. Mason looked at him and nodded.

"How is he doing now? Any signs of waking up yet? I need to ask him a couple of questions."

"He's still in shock and under medication. The doctor has said not to disturb him. He has been through a lot for more than a year now, Officer, please cut him some slack. He doesn't need it. I look at him and he looks like a stranger to me. His boyish looks are gone completely. I know I got to be thankful here mate, yet it shatters, shreds me to bits to see him like this."

"I understand, Mr. Mason. It is for his own safety. There might be another accomplice at play here. I need some clue to trail behind him. Mrs. Davis is also not doing good."

"What? There is someone else as well working with that crazy woman? I hope she rots in hell. That woman has been behind my son's kidnapping and sitting right under our very noses and pretending to sympathise with us. It's agonising that we could never see through her pretence," Mr. Mason said, gruffly and angrily. Just as he finished, Mrs. Mason and Macy strolled in anxiously towards the bed.

"Jack, how is our boy doing? What did the doctor say? Has he woken up at all?"

Jack walked up to them and gave them the update quietly. While Officer Scott was busy on his phone, idly his eyes caught a glimpse of the sibling reunion. There was an odd sense of something in her eyes—as Macy moved closer to her brother, there was longing in them for just a split second, and in half a blink there was a strangeness. Puzzled rather than intrigued, Officer Scott watched them from a distance, while the parents were busy whispering in hushed tones. At precisely that moment, Macy caught him staring at her, and within seconds she was holding her brother's hand gently and that look was washed off, replaced by a stream of tears. In that instant, Scott was confused, whether he had really seen something weird, or was it his imagination. Love can be all things, but most of all it is weird, he understood that seeing the pain, longing, and tears in her eyes.

Orange peels dried and toasted it smelled like when Ms. Murphy opened her eyes in the evening. The retiring stream of light tinted the stark white surroundings and jerked her into reality—of where she was and what had happened. She had detested hospitals ever since she was a kid. Something about it always weighed death higher on the scales than life. Suffering, pain, and helplessness were what picketed around this fence strongly. She tried to stir, but with all the cannulas pierced inside, she surrendered. Jerry, her boy, how was he, she wondered. Immediately she rang the bell to call the nurse. The nurse came along with Officer Scott by her side.

"Ms. Murphy, how are you feeling? You have indeed been a hero and saved the day, for sure."

"Not at all, Officer Scott. How are Jerry and Mrs. Davis now? Did you find out the whole story?"

"Not yet, we still don't know all the details. I was hoping you would be able to shed some light on it. Anything you remember from last night, what they might have told you?"

"Uh oh no. Actually, Jerry was too exhausted, I didn't bother him last night, although I was dying to. Mrs. Davis slept through the night, so I didn't get anything from her as well. I found it strange, that Jerry saved her and she was trying to kill him."

All of a sudden, there was some noise from behind the curtain. Some medicine bottles had spilled from a tray. Officer Scott sprinted to check who it was, but the person had disappeared or rather blended into the crowd—it was too late for him to catch. He wondered who was eavesdropping on their conversation. Or was it simply a nurse who had a mishap, he wondered.

"Don't worry. Jerry is safe now. Whoever it is, cannot go to attack him again, we have two guards standing at his door as well as that of Mrs. Davis. Mrs. Davis is not doing too well, I am afraid. Thank you for all your help. The doctor says you should get released tonight." Officer Scott nodded and left Ms. Murphy to rest.

The night ascended with an uncanny chill in the air, and strong winds whirred—as if soothsayers were murmuring a prophecy, willing for it to take place. The Redbarrow Woods looked unusually red—the trunks shone under the moonlit sky, as if a fresh coat of varnish had been applied, perked up, and alert. Even from the centre of the city—the Redbarrow hospital terrace. They say, every year-end has a day when the woods come alive—the intoxicating smell of wild flowers—musty and spicy, wafts far into the small town. It caresses; soft seductive tones are impregnated with secrets—some old, some new—all very true.

While the city sleeps soundly tonight, there are the wanderers who saunter around blithely. Tonight, an owl hoots on the window of a certain hospital room.

Someone pushed the door handles mutely, while the two officers snored on either side. The clock struck exactly two—and a masked person with black gloves removed the oxygen mask from the patient's face.

The patient started breathing heavily, unevenly, starving for air, while the masked person watched with bright eyes. A final breath left the patient's chest and a satisfied sigh from the spectator, who put the mask back on. Calmly, the masked person skimmed out of the room, unmasked, smiled, and nodded at a couple of nurses, walked out in the open, lit a cigarette, took a long drag, and grinned victoriously.

I have often wondered about death—what it would taste like, smell of, even look like. I was very young when our grandparents passed away, you remember, I don't really have any memory of it. It's dark, right? An abyss so unknown—yet the certainty of it is feared by all. It's like a force, that is so powerful, inevitable, and final. The finality of it horrifies us all. A curtain is raised and a curtain falls—one in which time deters, takes a detour to never cage us again. Like the whispers of the night, I wonder if it creeps up on us or stares deep and hard into our soul—sucking it up slowly, the angel of death wrings off the worldly attachments. Have you ever felt it so close, that your nose could perhaps touch it? Like you can taste it on the very tip of your tongue and it has a sharp taste—something surreal, a bitterness mixed with a pungency; it hits the soul, piercing like a dagger. This feels unreal, whispering to you while you lie peacefully on this bed. It took some convincing I dare say, Mama and Dad were quite reluctant to let me stay. In the end, I convinced them. They were tired and I could not have it any other way.

The dry specks of dawn appear with ringlets of pale cream clouds as I watch the borders of the night escape slowly. While the sweet smell of freshly laundered bed linen grows on me. Gently, I tuck the corner of the pillow snugly in the gap between my shoulder and my ear. Sleep comes to me almost instantaneously; for once I don't need pills. I never thought I would sleep so peacefully in a hospital; it certainly seems like an offence—given the amount of suffering and pain the patients suffer through the night. You see, the degree of sweetness is a very personal taste. What may seem too sweet or borderline bitter to you, may seem completely opposite to me. The point being, my night had just the right amount of sweetness, while I am certain the case might not be the same for very many people in this hospital.

I wake up to a lot of hustle and bustle—after my peaceful night, I guess I was prepared for a morning of mourning? Pfft! I am not making much sense, am I? Pretending to be asleep, what catches my attention is your voice. I take a quick peek, everyone surrounds you, while you sit with the backrest propping you up, sipping soup from Mama's hand. Chief Grant and Officer Scott are watching intently and listening to what you are saying.

"That day, after eating my food, I placed the empty plate on the ground near the door. Then I heard the door open slightly; something snapped inside me and I picked up the curtain rod and hit the person on the head. When the body fell inside, I realised who it was. Until then, I was not sure it was her, but then all my doubts faded away. I sat staring at her immobile, not knowing what to do honestly, because none of this was planned. My back was facing the door, so I was completely unaware that someone else stood there as well. Suddenly, I was hit, and immediately I fell unconscious. When I woke up, everything was pitch-black. The next thing I knew I was in the woods. Amidst the woods, my back was against a tree and someone was filling up mud into a hole. This time there were two people."

"Can you describe the two people? Did you get a clear view?" Chief Grant questioned.

By this time, I am wide awake. My first instinct is to jump out of bed and pounce on you with a hug.

"I am glad to see you too, Mace," you wince.

"I have missed you so much, Jerry, have you any idea? Please don't ever disappear again."

"If the siblings' reunion is over, might we continue here? With Mrs. Davis gone, we need to find the second accomplice in this act. Let me reiterate again—please, can you describe the two people trying to bury her? Have you ever seen them before?" Chief Grant probes impatiently.

"What? Mrs. Davis… what happened to her? What do you mean gone? How? When did it happen?" I ask, sounding shocked.

"She passed away in her sleep last night, the doctors believe. I have my doubts that someone took off the oxygen mask while those insolent guards slept through the night. We also have a lead on the person who kidnapped Jerry," Officer Scott mentions looking at me straight in the eye.

"Ms. Mason, where were you last night, can you tell me?"

"I was here, right next to Jerry, Officer," I say as innocently as possible.

He gets distracted as his phone rings and excuses himself without replying to me. Within a few minutes, Officer Scott comes back and announces, "We have the guy, Chief, he is at the station; I am going there right away to interrogate the hell out of him."

I push my thumbnail a little too hard into my little finger.

"Now, Jerry, can you continue with the description of the two people in the woods?" The Chief questions after Scott leaves the room.

"It was dark and foggy there, Chief. Honestly, I didn't get a clear view. I never did see their faces. The only thing clear to me from where I was hiding—one person was short and looked somewhat like a short girl, but I can't be too sure; the other one was surely a tall man. I was too scared to observe too much—petrified of being caught and killed. I held my breath while darkness embraced and concealed me, until finally they finished their burying and left."

"Wait! There is one thing I remember, the girl, her height, and frame were similar to Macy's," Jerry chimed in this revelation and everyone stared at Macy all together. Macy stared back at them nonplussed. Just at that moment, Officer Scott walked back in, dragging a tall scruffy man by his collar.

"Do you recognise this man, Ms. Mason?" he asked.

Chapter 26

I Will Return – To Me

I remember that day as clear as the skin of the flawless night sky. That winter day, one and a half years ago, when the weather was peach, not too cold, almost like a teenager experiencing, embracing, and evolving into youth. The sunlight was pale golden shimmery across the magnificent expanse, the clouds like soft, velvety lace sprawled around.

Dad was busy working in his study on some new campaign he had to present. You were in your room preparing for exams with a 'Don't disturb, Macy' sign on the door. Mama was baking her favourite apple crumble pie, humming to herself. The smell of caramelised apples with cinnamon wafted through my window. She was planning to go visit Mrs. Davis that day. I foraged through the kitchen to find something to nibble on.

It was a day when everyone just irrevocably felt good about themselves. It was a day, dreams didn't feel distant, just an arm's reach away. It was a day, that belied nothing at all. A day that grew on you like it would never end, making you weak only to rebuild the strength in hope. It was a day when this astronomical universe turned tiny in the palms of our hands into aspirations of each one of us—to cultivate, meander, and evolve into existence. We were alone in this journey—our struggles; there was an undeniable force weaving us all together to not feel lonely. A day that every broken piece found a piece of themselves that clicked them whole again. I dare say, a rare day indeed. Certainly, a day, nothing like the present, yet very much like now.

As they say, the Devil is always nearer than we imagine. Mama finished baking the pie and suggested that I go with her to Mrs. Davis's house. I had nothing really planned, so I agreed. Thinking about it now, I wish I had turned her down and simply lazed around at home. That was never meant to be, eh? The streets were chequered with people of all kinds. Everyone basking in a bit of this glory, I would say. There was a child with a triumphant grin on his face standing by the ice cream parlour licking his lips as he whispered to the man for an extra scoop of ice cream. Not very far, Mrs. Smith was outside the bustling Baked & Iced Café waving her hand at us. A group of friends were cycling across with picnic baskets and camping gear.

Shortly, we arrived at Mrs. Davis's house; she greeted us warmly at the door and Mama gave her the pie. She was elated. We were welcomed into her house with the smell of lamb stew and sauteed vegetables. While both of them chatted, I excused myself to find a book. I wandered far into the house and soon I found myself in her study. She never really allowed anybody near her study—making it all the more alluring to us. I was undeniably tempted to enter and explore it—I mean, what could there be that she was being so secretive about all the time? My inquisitiveness got the better of my conscience and I thought to myself, a quick look will not do any harm. Besides they were so busy chatting, I would whisk in and out and they won't even be able to tell, I decided.

When I entered the study, it smelled of cappuccino and scrambled eggs on toast. The study had a plethora of stationery; it was almost like a stationery shop. I was so intrigued, fascinated, and engrossed that I never wanted to leave the study. After admiring her collection of pencils, pens, erasers, highlighters, glue sticks, letter pads, envelopes, and what not—I arrived at her study table. There was an incomplete letter on a beige letter paper with tiny pink tulips at the end, sprouting irregularly. The handwriting looked like printed calligraphy; it was the most beautiful handwritten letter I had ever encountered. It was not something I could resist reading at all. So, I did read it. At first, I never understood to who it was addressed or about whom she was writing.

My hunger grew ravenous. I rummaged through the drawers and found all the recent entries—they were from the time she started noticing your similarities to her son. The letters were full of emotions and so tender—with an underlying tone of yearning, which grew stronger and stronger. I couldn't control my tears; it was a foreign terrain so endearing to me. I don't know when it happened; her longing manifested into a personal one. The raw yearning for my parents' attention drove hard into her yearning for her son. And then, boom! A plan started weaving in that devious little mind of mine. I was certain—me coming into her study, reading her letters, and finding the connection was not a mere accident. No, it was beyond the role of fate—it was destiny.

A destiny that was irreversible, one that had me in the driving seat. Hadn't I longed for it enough? Hadn't she mourned into insanity? We deserved a piece of peace just like everybody else did. I couldn't possibly do it in front of Mama, I had to find the right time. After carefully putting all the letters back in place, I took a twirl around and rechecked. Once I was satisfied, I walked backwards out through the door and was about to close the door when I bumped into someone behind me. I froze. Being caught in an act of deception always feels like a mousse that turned flat in spite of the gelatin. It wriggles and simply plops unappetizingly. For the next few seconds, I didn't know what to do. Then I heard her crossly question me…

"What are you doing in my study, Macy, dear? You know I don't like people intruding into my privacy."

"I apologise, Mrs. D; I was just wandering and didn't realise I had come so far out. I promise I didn't disturb anything," I said batting my lashes innocently.

She nodded, definitely looking unconvinced. I didn't give her much choice either. Mama greeted us at the dining table. Through lunch, everything seemed to have settled down. We chattered, ate, and laughed heartily as Mrs. D poured velvety jus over the braised lamb and we nibbled on the vegetables sauteed to perfection. In my mind, I was busy knitting a plan for execution as soon as possible. After lunch, I told Mama I would stay back for a bit, I was still in two minds about a book. While she agreed readily, Mrs. Davis looked at me slightly suspiciously. However, she never did protest about it to Mama.

When I finally got Mrs. Davis alone, I pretended the selection of a book – To Kill a Mockingbird. Yes, this was the very book on which I had scribbled that phrase 'I Will Return - To Me'. I read that phrase in one of her letters and it stuck with me—what better way to start than starting with a phrase, and I could copy your handwriting seamlessly. Also, no one knew about it except you of course. Before I proceed, I want to make one thing very clear. While I planned and plotted, I never did want to harm anybody, least of all you and Mrs. D. It was supposed to be a strategy that would end both our individual yearnings. The biggest scratch in my plan was that I didn't realise Mama, Dad, and me would miss you so much. Overwhelmed by emotions, I completely missed that bit somehow. Longing is like a rainbow, so enchanting, and alluring that one easily believes if they acquire it, there will be a pot of gold at the end, and that we would never be in need of anything else. That is not how it works; I realise it now. We paid Steven Jackson (a guard gone rogue), to break through the window and tie you unconscious. The rest of the plan only Mrs. Davis and the thief coordinated; I didn't want to know.

Mrs. Davis was listening with tears running down her cheeks; she couldn't believe her dream was about to come true. One that seemed so far-fetched, one that she believed would remain a dream and would simply die with her last breaths. While she asked many questions, she somehow found it hard to believe why a doting sister would like to be estranged from her brother. The thing was, I couldn't explain that bit to her honestly. You see, I was afraid if things went south, I would be held responsible for the whole thing. I didn't want that. So, I wired my reasoning around her yearning. That I was so moved by her letters, the deep scars of yearning dug something into me and I wanted her to heal. My brother is the dearest and kindest soul, he would love to heal her aching heart and both of you would go away to her hometown after that. I watched the way you spent time with her, you cared for her too. She fell for it—moved by my words.

There were many loopholes in our plan. Much as I tried, I was still a teenager in all its entirety. One of the biggest flaws was that we never planned an evacuation out of this mess. After the kidnapping was done, I instructed her not to even tell me where she would be hiding you. A moment of weakness, or if I were to be suspected, I could never trail it back to her. The scruffy Steven Jackson (a guard gone rogue) we hired for the deed was quite well experienced in this field; I had met him once, and so he had identified me quite easily to the cops, unfortunately. The timeline between the kidnapping and finally leaving for good was not discussed. We simply assumed, after hearing her sob story, you would accept her and live with her. I imagined you would come to visit us at times. Absurd as it may sound, in the madness of the moment, I didn't think straight. You were evidently so fond of her always, it didn't seem like an astronomical task.

Unfortunately, she was petrified and simply never got around to confessing it all and embracing you with her true intentions. Perhaps, her heart was touched by the fact that you were living with her and that weakened her resolve to continue 'just one more day' that simply never ended. The cops were getting closer; sniffing around for blood. Things started getting uncomfortable, and stuffy, and I was getting fidgety. I was done leading everyone astray with that 'phrase'. Too much time had passed already. The months started turning from green to orange to white, fallen leaves can never be attached back to their roots. I was waiting, that you would appear one day and just start behaving like her son.

The wait turned greyish to black, there were thunder rumblings outside and inside my head. But I could never discuss it with her, that was the pact we had made. To be careful, never to let the mist of our conspiracy dampen the walls even. I grew restless from the outside—started hallucinating scenes that had been already executed. Panic lunged at me from most unexpected directions; I had absolutely no one to fall back on. So, one day, reluctantly I decided to visit her, and confront her with what she planned to do. Of course, Officer Scott came in the same day to ask about her son. That was it for me. I started to panic. Desperately I needed another plan.

Sometimes, we plan to escape only to get caught in them—those plans are called rage plans, they simply fizzle out like a feeble day's rays of the sun. Burnt and gorged on by the intensity of this, I felt like an animal trapped in a cage. I needed to disengage and act. Out of sheer desperation, I called the scruffy man again to help me carry Mrs. D and you. Yes, it was me, who had hit you. I found myself burying her instead of you, when I hadn't even planned on it. I believe I left you there because some part of the sister in me still lived deep inside. Much as I would have liked otherwise. You see certain acts in life come out of some deep dungeon buried in us. In those moments we marvel—are left between undefinable lines of darkness and light.

Sitting in this mental health facility room, it is easy for me to share all this with you. Over the year, it has become easy for me to talk to you—when you are not even there. The doctors are nice; they try hard here. I am far from telling this story to them or to anyone else for that matter. Stark-white walls stare at me—trying to judge me. The single bed in the room seems treacherous. I don't trust the vindictive sisters here too, they smell evil. Some days are easy, others graze past bitingly. I try to behave my best when you come to meet me. The pain grows intensely every day, when the only two people I yearn for, seldom turn up. You on the contrary are a regular here. After all that I did, you still love me. I can see it in your eyes and feel so much more pathetic about myself. I guess that is my biggest punishment.

Epilogue

Closure comes like a surprise guest; invited yet unexpected, knocking on the door, and it hosts me most graciously in my very own dilapidated state. This day lies witness, that I have returned to me. The shadow between light and darkness that I was clinging to has been lifted. I feel no suffocation and no threat anymore. My constant feeling on the edge has found a home. A home that has returned to me. One that I had been starving, desperate, and angry for. The four walls that used to make me feel like a stranger, no more do. The three people—my family come to visit me as frequently as permitted.

Forgiveness, there is so much force in that word, like a sigh that needs tremendous effort to let out. Break it into two syllables and you get a gentler hold on it—for and giveness. Can you feel it on your tongue? The stages of this word manifest on many textures: some are see-through, you know, like a flimsy fabric we wear, others are thick, velvety to touch with a scent of Gardenia, sultry, that settles on you like a memory. They have come to terms to forgive me. I wipe away my tears, tears feel cold on my flushed cheeks, and my hands grip the bed stands tightly. Only I really don't know which manifestation of it has been bestowed on me. There is an agony I suppress; it itches my throat impatiently, trying to escape. I hold it back.

Six years have passed since that day at the hospital. Dad did hire the top lawyer for me, who won the case. He proved I was on medications and a juvenile. They sent me to the facility. At the facility, I don my best behaviour and hide under my mask, as I learned how to hold the reins on my real feelings long ago. Everything blurs, only they are clearer than ever before. Eventually, they clear my slate and say a huge improvement—theoretically cured and discharged. I almost laugh in their faces.

I am sitting on the terrace with you—eating oranges; on a couch, and my legs up on a wooden stool. What has led us to this may have been rough and has marked us all with bruises. Every time I look at you, you smile back. At times, I notice the raw, vacant frustration in your eyes—from the corner of my eyes; when you think no one can see. The shock of it plunges you into some place indescribable. Perhaps, the loopholes in the case, that the police were never able to solve, haunt you. For instance, Mrs. D, did she really pass away in her sleep, or was there more to it? Sometimes, I wonder if you know more than you reveal. Then, I brush away that thought and convince myself it was not possible. Otherwise, wouldn't things be different? Love, in all its capacity, is that stranger you find all so familiar, when it becomes all too familiar you find it strange.

Acknowledgements

In the name of Allah, the Most Beneficent and
the Most Merciful

When I finally got to this page, I felt tiny droplets of nervousness hit me. Honestly, this whole journey feels surreal. You can never do complete justice to thanking the Almighty and his mysterious messengers who assist you in different walks of life. Before starting, I would like to apologise for any names I may have missed—completely unintentional.

I want to start by thanking Vijayalakshmi Menon for being brave enough to read my manuscript (fun fact —she was the first one who read my manuscript), for her constructive feedback and invaluable inputs. I want to thank Charmine Joseph for holding my finger and starting this collaboration with Notion Press so smoothly. Shijoy John for bearing with my impatience, and doubts, and still delivering much more than promised. I would like to thank the whole team of Notion Press for pulling off this project so smoothly.

I would like to thank the team of YourQuote and all my fellow writers who inspire me immensely in this journey called writing. My friends—school and college, for just letting me be my crazy self and hone my imagination. My colleagues at work for helping me define my dreams and pushing me towards it. I would like to thank my teachers and mentors at work who inspired, encouraged, and motivated me tremendously.

My mother for kindling the writer in me—by introducing the joyous world of reading and being an unbreakable shield of protection constantly. My father for leaving behind abundant and unending love that became my greatest strength. I would like to thank my dearest siblings—Sadia and Shahryar without whom in my life—I would never have understood sibling love. My dear aunt, Dr. Rukeya for her invaluable input for the hospital scene. My entire extended family, uncles, aunts, cousins, grandparents, and in-laws for chipping in my imagination at some point in life.

I would like to thank my husband—Danish, for being a constant source of support, love, patience, and encouragement in pursuing my dream. My dearest children—Rayyan and Barakah for bearing with me patiently all the times when I had to dedicate myself to my book and for being super excited over mommy becoming an author.

To every individual, whosoever touched my life even for a brief few seconds, my heartiest gratitude to them—for my characters coloured a shade lighter or darker because of them. Lastly, to all of you reading my book, sending you my deepest gratitude for arriving at my bookport and flying this tale with me as your captain.

www.ingramcontent.com/pod-product-compliance
Lightning Source LLC
LaVergne TN
LVHW041207150826
845673LV00001B/312

* 9 7 9 8 8 8 8 6 9 3 4 9 0 *